Samuel French Acting Edi

Lydia

by Octavio Solis

SAMUEL FRENCH

ISBN 978-0-573-69816-3

www.concordtheatricals.com
www.concordtheatricals.co.uk

FOR PRODUCTION INQUIRIES

UNITED STATES AND CANADA
info@concordtheatricals.com
1-866-979-0447

UNITED KINGDOM AND EUROPE
licensing@concordtheatricals.co.uk
020-7054-7200

Each title is subject to availability from Concord Theatricals Corp., depending upon country of performance. Please be aware that *LYDIA* may not be licensed by Concord Theatricals Corp. in your territory. Professional and amateur producers should contact the nearest Concord Theatricals Corp. office or licensing partner to verify availability.

This work is published by Samuel French, an imprint of Concord Theatricals Corp.

Please refer to page 83 for further copyright information.

LYDIA was first produced by the Denver Center Theater Company (Kent Thompson, artistic director) at the Space Theatre in Denver, Colorado on January 24, 2008. The performance was directed by Juliette Carrillo, with sets by Antje Ellermann, costumes by Christal Weatherly, lighting by Charles R. MacLeod, original music by Chris Webb, sound by Kimberly Fuhr, and fight direction by Geoffrey Kent. The production stage manager was Lyle Raper. The cast was as follows:

CECI .... Onahoua Rodriguez
MISHA .... Carlo Alban
RENE .... Rene Millan
ROSA .... Catalina Maynard
CLAUDIO .... Ricardo Guitierrez
ALVARO .... Christian Barillas
LYDIA .... Stephanie Beatriz

CHARACTERS

CECI – the sister, 17

MISHA – the younger brother, 16

RENE – the older brother, 19

ROSA – the mother

CLAUDIO – the father

ALVARO – the cousin, 22

LYDIA – the maid

TIME

The early 70s, in winter.

PLACE

The living room of Flores home in El Paso, Texas. Early 70s furnishings. A sofa with a coffee table, its surface scratched and stained. An old La-Z-Boy facing the TV. A stereo console with a set of headphones attached. A door to the front porch. A darkened hallway to the bedrooms. An entry to the kitchen. In the foreground by the TV, a small mattress with pillows and stuffed animals.

CECI'S CONDITION

For most of the play, Ceci lies on her mattress locked in her body in a semi-vegetative state. Her body's muscles rigid, her hands curled and fingers knuckled, she undergoes degrees of spasticity which come and go in ways that score the play. Her voice is fallen back into her throat and her eyes unfocussed, her powers of expression are utterly buried in a neurological prison.

ACT 1

*(**AT RISE:** The living room of the Flores home.* **CLAUDIO** *slumps on the La-Z-Boy watching TV. Ironing his white shirts and pants is his wife* **ROSA.** *In her mattress lies* **CECI** *in her pajamas, a long thin scar rising from her eyebrow and disappearing into her hairline. She lies very still, her eyes on the flickering light of the TV. After a moment, an awareness dawns on her and she starts.)*

CECI. She touched me and I flew. Touched my fault-line. And I flew. With her hand, laid holy water on my scar. And I flew on wings of glass. My body *como una* bird racing with the moon on a breath of air. Flying out of range of pain, purpose, this thing we call *Vida,* soaring into the blueness of memory, closing my eyes for the thud to come.

(She closes her eyes. Opens them.)

I wake to this. Life inside my life. No wings, no glass, no moon. Only *Loteria* which means Bingo which means chance which means play. So I play the cards into view.

(She looks down at her arms and legs curling under her as a light falls on her mattress.)

A card with me printed, *La Vida Cecilia,* rag doll thumbing the stitching in her head, forming the words in her vegetable tongue, what happened to me, *porque no puedo* remember, I must remember.

(The light bears down on **CLAUDIO.***)*

There. A card called El Short-Order Cook. Broken man drowning in old *rancheras* and TV. I hear *voces antiguas* calling his name, Claudio, my poor Papi Claudio in your personal winter, drowning out the will of *Mami* saying come with me across the *rio,* give up that lie you thought was you and live mine, live American with me. So the dish ran away with the greasy spoon and a girl jumped over the moon but you don't spikka the English, only the word No, which in Spanish means No, No at work in bed in your dreams in your *cantos perdidos.*

(The light shifts to **ROSA**, *ironing clothes and muttering silent prayers to herself.)*

CECI. *(cont.) Aqui,* the Mami Rosa card, dressmaker of flying girls, sewing up my unfinished seams; a beautiful woman losing beauty by the day, see it gathered at her feet like old panty hose, *ay Ama!* You were Rosie Flores, clerk for the County, making your life here, Anglo words like lazy moths tumbling out your mouth, you were *toda* proud, but now. You're Rosa Reborn holy-rolling me to sleep with the prayers of your new church. Your prayers for us to be family which hasn't really been family since they stopped putting cork in soda bottle caps.

*(***RENE** *comes in from down the hall. He goes to the front door and retrieves the day's mail. He goes over it carefully.)*

CECI. *Ayy.* My wild card, *El Carnal Mayor,* Rene, my elder volcano, bustin' noses just by looking at 'em, both hands fulla middle fingers for the whole world, checking every day for hate mail, but always *nada.* Cars go by and honk *Puto-Puto-Rene-Puto!* but cowards, my brother is invincible.

(He throws the mail on the coffee table and stares at **CECI.***)*

The army recruiter don't want you, huh, not like those other flag-draped *Chicanos* on our block, even those that come back alive look like they gave up the ghost, that's kinda what you want, that damned ghost taken out of you. 'Cause you're all messed up with some hard-core macho shit nobody gets.

(He finally looks at **CECI** *and slowly comes to her.)*

CECI. *(cont.) Andale,* plant a kiss on my head like that saint in church with the chipped nose –

(He kisses her and leaves out the front door.)

dry-kiss and move away. *Simon, carnal,* Before the disgust starts to show.

*(***MISHA*** enters with his books. Flops down on the couch.)*

Misha? *¿Eres tu?* Card with the inscription Little Shit. *Carnalito* Misha bringing to my *nariz* fragrances of the street the school his body, yes, the musk of you coming of age, coming into yourself, coming all *over* yourself. I hear your little secrets like crystals of salt in the pockets of your eyes, sad-boy Misha, sad for me, for us, the things that darken the day, King and Kennedy, the killings of students, the killings of Nam – *Mi familia.* All sad and wounded cause of somethin'. Somethin' that broke. I gotta read my scar for the story, it's in there, I know it! *¡Aguas!* I see her. The girl that touched me…her face in a mirror looking back… showing me her own sccc – ggghn mmm her- own – ssccrrmmgfmhm...

MISHA. Mom, what's wrong with Ceci?

ROSA. *Alomejor* she went poo-poo.

MISHA. She doesn't smell like it.

ROSA. Maybe she wants her therapy. Could you do it, Misha? I'm pressing your father's shirts for work.

*(***MISHA*** sits by* **CECI** *and runs her through a repertoire of delicate physical exercises, shifting her position from time to time.)*

MISHA. *Orale, carnala.* Let's get the blood pumping.

ROSA. *Con cariño,* okay?

MISHA. Always gentle, Ama. Hey Dad.

ROSA. He can't hear you.

MISHA. Dad!

ROSA. *¿Que te dije?* What are you doing home so early? Don't you have practice?

MISHA. *(as he rubs* **CECI***'s arms and hands)* I dropped out of the squad. Football ain't my game. You hear that, Dad? I'm a wuss and I don't understand what all those little circles and arrows mean. I can't hear the quarterback in the huddle. He grunts uhh twenty-uhhh on huuu – uuhh! But I go on huuu and Coach yells at me. At the scrimmage today, a touchdown got called back on account of I was off-sides. I told them it wasn't my fault. I told them we need enunciation in the huddle. In the showers they all towel-whipped my bare *ass.*

ROSA. Watch your language.

MISHA. So you know what, Dad, I quit. I turned in my equipment and walked. I'm sorry, Mom. I just feel I'm needed here.

ROSA. It's okay, *mijo.* I never liked you playing with those *brutos.* You're my special boy. That's why I named you Misha.

MISHA. You named me Miguel.

ROSA. But after I saw that Baryshnikov on TV, I started calling you Misha.

MISHA. I don't even like ballet.

ROSA. The point is a brown boy named Misha in El Paso is special. I got my hopes pinned all over you like dollars.

MISHA. Is there anything to eat?

ROSA. There's *albondigas* on the stove.

MISHA. Meatballs? From last night?

ROSA. They're a little dried out, but still good. You want some?

MISHA. *¿Jefita?*

*(***ROSA** *looks. He opens* **CECI***'s arms wide.)*

I *wuv* you this much.

ROSA. *Sangron.*

(She laughs and goes into the kitchen.)

CECI. Huuh onhuu-uuh.

MISHA. You sound like my quarterback.

CECI. Shhghgm.

MISHA. The truth is when I'm on the field, I don't pay attention. I watch the yellowing grass and the zip-zip-zip of the sprinklers and the clouds making ponytails in the sky.

CECI. Uhh. Ghhh. Gngngm.

MISHA. Mom. There's something different about her.

ROSA. What?

MISHA. I dunno. Something. Are you still giving her her meds?

ROSA. *(returning with a bowl of meatballs)* Of course!

MISHA. 'Cause I know you don't sometimes, Mom. I know how you "forget" sometimes.

ROSA. I don't forget, never!

MISHA. Where are they? Where're the pills? How much did you give her today? How much, Mom!

ROSA. *Oye,* it's not drugs she needs but faith! Faith! *Mijo,* the doctors said it was over, remember, she's a vegetable *para siempre,* they said. What are these pills supposed to do then?

MISHA. Give me the pills. Or I'm telling him.

ROSA. Tell him. *Andale. Dile todo.*

*(**MISHA** turns to his father.* ***CLAUDIO*** *takes off his headphones and stands.)*

CLAUDIO. *Que paso, Miguel. ¿Como te va en el* football?

MISHA. Good.

ROSA. I'm almost done here. Just a few more shirts.

CLAUDIO. *¿Como?*

ROSA. *Nomas estas camisas, Viejo.*

CLAUDIO. *Miguel, una cerveza.*

*(**MISHA** nods gravely as* ***CLAUDIO*** *goes down the hall to the bathroom.)*

ROSA. Praise God.

MISHA. I wish you'd keep your religion to yourself. It's not doing Ceci any good.

ROSA. *Oyeme,* Misha. When your sister got hurt, I prayed to the *Virgen Santa, la Patronesa de todos los Mexicanos. La Virgen de Guadalupe* herself. And she failed me. That's when I knew. Us *Catolicos,* we worship the wrong things. Idols can't make miracles. Only God. So I go to a church with no other gods but God.

MISHA. Has that done her any good? Has it?

ROSA. Today. While your father was sleeping. You know what I did? I took her to Our Church of the Nazarene.

MISHA. What? You took her to those holy rollers? Are you kidding me?

ROSA. Misha, she loved it. All the peoples adored her. And Pastor Lujan himself baptized her.

MISHA. What?

ROSA. He put her in this big glass tub and laid his hand on her, *mijo.* Right here where her precious brains came out, and he prayed to God for her soul. He dipped her backward in the water and her face came alive! Eyes bright as nickels and her mouth wide open, taking in the light of heaven! Pastor Lujan said very clearly: Cecilia, prepare you! Your redemption is knocking on your head. And he took her pills and poured them all into the same tub.

MISHA. Oh no…

ROSA. He said we don't need them anymore! He said it's evil in our hearts that makes her sick.

MISHA. No more saving her soul. I mean it. Leave her soul alone.

ROSA. Don't you lecture me on how I care for *mija*! Who stays home with her day and night, changing her when she needs to go, making her special food, rubbing her joints *y todo*? Who?

MISHA. I help.

ROSA. *Por favor,* Misha. You're in school all day.

MISHA. I know.

ROSA. Well, I know more. Nothing happens without me in this house. I see to our needs. That's how come we're getting a maid.

MISHA. A maid? Like to clean the house?

ROSA. To clean the house, to cook the food, to watch your sister. I asked your Tia Mirna, and she said her maid knows this *chavala* from *Jalisco* who just came over and she needs work and she's cheap.

MISHA. What about you?

ROSA. They called from the county office and told me my old position is available if I want it. Well, I want it. I'm tired of staying in this house all day. Plus we need the money.

MISHA. Is she legal?

ROSA. I don't ask about such things. I just ask her to come tomorrow.

MISHA. Tomorrow? Dammit, why didn't you tell me?

ROSA. I did. Watch your tongue. Last week. I mentioned it at dinner. But you never listen. You and your brother only hear what you want to hear.

*(**CLAUDIO** returns from the bathroom.)*

CLAUDIO. *¿Y mi cerveza?*

MISHA. Mom *dice que* we're gonna have a maid, *una criada.*

CLAUDIO. *Asi lo quiere.*

MISHA. *¿Y tu, que quieres?*

CLAUDIO. *Mi pinche cerveza.*

(He sits and puts his headphones on again. **MISHA** *watches him.)*

ROSA. You heard him.

MISHA. What am I, his *mesero*?

(She glares at him. **MISHA** *goes off to the kitchen and reenters with a can of beer.)*

Ask yourself, Mom. Do we really want this? Do we really want a stranger coming into our house?

ROSA. What's wrong with our house? What don't you want her to see? What are you ashamed of, Misha? Your sister?

MISHA. Not her.

ROSA. I promise you. When she comes here, she will find a close, caring Mexican *familia* trying to make it in this blessed country.

CLAUDIO. *(impatiently waiting for his beer)* Miguel…

ROSA. Get over your *verguenza* and give your father his beer.

MISHA. Mom…

ROSA. Do it, Miguel.

*(**CLAUDIO** suddenly gets up, takes the beer and slaps **MISHA** across the face.)*

CLAUDIO. *Tres veces te lo pedí, cabrón. Tres veces.*

*(He sits, rips off the pull-tab and drops it on the floor by **CECI**. He watches TV as **MISHA**'s eyes well with tears.)*

ROSA. *¿Que te dije?* Pick up that pull-tab before your sister cuts herself with it.

*(**CECI** turns to speak to **MISHA** as he picks up the pull-tab, his cheek reddening with the heat of the blow, and goes to his room.)*

CECI. It's okay, *carnalito.* I hear your face clapping against the way things are, and I know it hurts, 'cause I feel my face smashing against the mad will of God. I remember that, Misha, like I remember we can't let the swelling block us off, we gotta believe that it passes, bro, it passes. Sure as day passes into night.

*(Suddenly, night. **CECI** lying on her mattress. Headlights swivel across the window drapes as **RENE** comes in the front door. He stands and waits in the dark until his breath is even. He watches **CECI** with a mix of fear and contempt. **MISHA** enters.)*

RENE. Any mail?

MISHA. No. *(notices his bloody knuckles)* Vato.

RENE. It's nothing.

MISHA. Nothing. You're bleeding.

RENE. What's a little *molé.* You should see them.

MISHA. Are you drunk too?

RENE. It helps, don't you think? So you and me and some Buds?

MISHA. We're out. And it's too late to hit the Circle K.

RENE. I don't need no shit Circle fucking K, goddammit. I need me some *pisto. Watcha.*

(He reaches under the cushions of the La-Z-Boy. A fifth of Southern Comfort.)

MISHA. Whoa.

RENE. Papa's gotta brand new bag.

MISHA. How'd you know it was there?

RENE. *Ese,* he sits in that chair all *pinchi* day like he's incubating a fucking *huevo. Andale, tragito!*

(They slug some down.)

Nothing like a little *pisto* to smooth out the rough edges of a bad night.

MISHA. Was it a bad night?

RENE. Hell no, it was a good night. We kicked some ass.

MISHA. What did you do?

RENE. We kicked some ass.

MISHA. How about a little more detail, *ese*?

RENE. We kicked some fucking ass.

MISHA. Rene.

RENE. You're too young. You don't get the vibe. This is me, Joey and Sergio taking on the *pinchi* world.

MISHA. Joey and Sergio? Those pussies?

RENE. *No mames, guey!* These are my *camaradas*! Besides, we need Joey's van for the ceremony.

MISHA. What ceremony?

RENE. *Pos,* first we chug back some brew for a couple hours, listen to some Sabbath, toke a little *mota* for courage. Then we think of cheerleaders and whack off a little till we're nice and hard and then we hit the road.

MISHA. And kick some ass.

RENE. Fuckin' A.

MISHA. I heard it was some *cholos* last night.

RENE. Tough little fuckers in training for prison, gang tats y *toda la madre.* We kicked their ass. *Dame.*

(He drinks. Some red and white lights flash by the window.)

¡Trucha! Get down! Down!

MISHA. Shit, Rene! Is that the cops?

RENE. Just be quiet and keep your head down.

*(***RENE** *peeks through the drapes till the lights pass.)*

MISHA. What the fuck happened? You better tell me or I'm gonna wake up Mom and tell her the cops are after you.

RENE. *Calmantes montes,* narc. I'll tell you, but only as a cautionary tale for you not to put your ass where it's likely to be kicked, *me entiendes*?

*(***MISHA** *nods.)*

We took on some GI's.

MISHA. Shit. Oh shit.

RENE. Fresh outa Ft. Bliss. We went up the mountain on Scenic Drive and pulled over by these cars. And there they were, a *gringo salado* and a couple *negros.* We just approached them like some tourists up to see the sights, you know? They offered us some beers and were really nice to us. But these *fags,* Meesh, you gotta watch out for them.

MISHA. How come.

RENE. Just 'cause I say so. Anyway, the *gringo* puts his hand on my knee so I gotta cut him with a right hook that snaps his head back. Joey and Serge lay into the others and man, it's on. We lay into these jive-turkey motherfuckers with basic-training biceps. Serge is swinging this bat on their heads and Joey's got nunchucks and blood is shootin' volcanic all over the place.

MISHA. You hit 'em with bats? What if you put 'em in the hospital with like brain damage or something?

RENE. Hey, don't talk brain damage. Not in front of her. Pay your penance, fuck.

(**RENE** *offers the bottle and* **MISHA** *drinks.)*

MISHA. I don't get it, man. Why are you doing this shit? When are you gonna go to college or get a real job?

RENE. I gotta job.

MISHA. Car detailing at Earl Scheib? You're smarter than that.

RENE. What's the pinche point, bro? I'm gonna get drafted anyway.

MISHA. Is that what you're looking for in the mail? Your draft notice? *Ese*, your birthdate's not due in the lottery till next year.

RENE. *No mames, guey.*

MISHA. If you're so anxious about it, if you wanna kill someone, go enlist like Alvaro.

RENE. I ain't that stupid.

MISHA. Neither is he. He came back with a bronze star. Gung-ho guys like him always seem to make out okay.

RENE. Varo's too hot-shit for us now. Back three months and he still hasn't come to our *chante.*

MISHA. Mom says he's been focusing on getting some steady work.

CECI. Varo. Varo Varo Varo.

MISHA. I know this much. War keeps going like it is, I'm gonna have to go to Canada.

RENE. Canada? Why truck all the way up there, Mexico's right there, you dope!

MISHA. Well, on TV, that's where they all say they're going! Canada!

RENE. 'Cause they're white, stupid! Canada! You're a trip. What are you doing up?

MISHA. I couldn't sleep. I had this dream. Hey, you know Mom's hiring some chick to take care of Ceci?

RENE. Old news, bro.

MISHA. She's coming tomorrow to cook and do the wash. Tell you one thing, she ain't touching my clothes.

RENE. You got some stains in your *chones* you don't want her to see?

MISHA. Shut up.

RENE. Haha! Is that what you had? A wet dream?

MISHA. Cut it out. It was scary as shit. We were kids, you, me Alvaro, and Ceci, all alone in this house.

RENE. What happened?

MISHA. We were playing like we used to. We put chairs all over the living room, down the hall, covered them up with sheets and we crawled under pretending we were ants in our tunnels. We scurried from chamber to chamber, touching heads lightly, making those little tee-tee sounds in ant-language. Ceci's eyes full of joy. She had those pearl earrings she got for her *Quinceañera.* We saw her go off with this shiny key in her mouth. I think it was a key. It looked like a key. Her shadow against the sheet one second, and the next, gone. We went through the tunnels looking for her, but we couldn't find her. I wanted to call out "Ceci", but you said use ant-language. I couldn't think of the words for please come back, and I went all through the tunnel, looking for her. I woke up absolutely freaked. I came out here and saw the invisible lines of the tunnels all over the floor.

RENE. I'm sackin' out before the old man comes home. You shouldn't be dreaming shit like that, Misha.

(He returns the bottle to the cushion seam and goes.)

CECI. Gghn.

*(**MISHA** goes to **CECI** and looks into her eyes. He gently pries her mouth open. He looks inside. He lets her go and then walks off to bed.)*

CECI. *(cont.)* You won't find nothin' down there but spit and the words to *Cielito Lindo.* I feel it coming around again like a Mexican yoyo, little ball up on its string and plop right into the bowl of my heart.

*(**CLAUDIO** enters from the shadows in white shirt and trousers with his paper hat.)*

It's the night of my race with the moon. He comes in his fry-cook whites to my room, wearing that white paper hat like a general. I'm at the threshold of my *senorita*-hood, pretending to sleep, feeling his raw breath in my ear singing for the last time…

(He sings softly as he opens his hands and reveals a pair of pearl earrings.)

CLAUDIO. *De la sierra morena*
Cielito lindo vienen bajando
Un par de ojitos negros
Cielito lindo de contrabando

Ese lunar que tienes
Cielito lindo junto a la boca
No se lo des a nadie
Cielito lindo que a mí me toca

Ay ay ay ay
Canta y no llores
Porque cantando se alegran
Cielito lindo los corazones

(He gets up and slowly walks off into the darkness.)

CECI. A tear from each eye turned to pearl and laid on my pillow to make the moon jealous. Oh what is this yearning inside? What does it mean?

*(The next day. **ROSA** comes in dressed for work, fussing about, straightening up the house with a minimum of noise.)*

ROSA. *¡Ay Diosito diosito!* Where is this girl? *¡Ya son las ocho y media! ¡Ay, que nervio!*

CECI. Ghghnn.

ROSA. Okay, okay, I'm coming! *Ya ya.* I know, I know. This house smells like a *cantina*! What were these *barbaros* up to last night, Ceci?

CECI. Gghhn.

(She goes to the kitchen and quickly returns with a bowl of oatmeal. She sits and stirs the oatmeal around with a spoon.)

ROSA. *Ta bien, mija.* I know everything in this house. I know they were drinking. I know Rene was fighting again. But what can I do? He does what he does. *¿Tienes apetito por some oatmeal? Ven.*

(She holds **CECI** *as she raises a spoonful of oatmeal.)*

Oh, *espera.* We forgot grace.

(She holds **CECI***'s hands and closes her eyes.)*

Dear Lord Jesus Holy Father, we submit this meal today for your blessing that we may not want and pray for your mercy, for You made us in order to love us and as we take this meal please forgive our sins and heal us first in our *corazones* so that the body may follow. In your most precious and holy name, Amen.

(She guides the spoon into her mouth.)

Not too hot? Good.

(She continues to talk as she feeds her.)

My pretty girl. Even the accident couldn't keep this body from growing. It's my body, Ceci, the body I used to have. The hip-huggers and halter tops I would have bought you! *¡Lastima de tu quinceañera!* I made with my own Singer the whitest most beautiful dress with lace running all the way down the sleeve to the wrist. Like a Disney *Chicana* you would look! Regal and sexy, but definitely chaste. You would save that *cosita* for after your wedding. *Pero ahora, pobre mija.* It's just a dead flower on you now.

*(***CECI** *jerks and thrusts the bowl of oatmeal all over herself and her mother.)*

CECI. GGGhhhmmm!

ROSA. *¡AY! ¡¡Cecilia Rosario! ¡Que has hecho!* Look at my dress! *¡Inutil!*

*(**CECI** flails madly about. **LYDIA** appears at the door, bag in hand.)*

LYDIA. *¿Señora?*

ROSA. *Oh. Si, si, si. ¿Eres la muchacha de Jalisco?*

LYDIA. Yes.

ROSA. *¿Hablas Ingles?*

LYDIA. *Si, Señora – o sea…*Yes, I would prefer. I am learning.

ROSA. *Entonces,* come in. Come in, please.

*(She enters. **CECI** is still angrily flailing her arms.)*

CECI. Ggnnhf!

LYDIA. *Perdón, pero me perdí.* I…. I….got lost…..

CECI. GGGhn!

ROSA. It's okay, okay, I understand.

LYDIA. Let me. I help. You go wash.

*(**LYDIA** puts down her bag and goes to **CECI**. She cleans her with her napkin.)*

ROSA. No, no, please, she's very hard to –

LYDIA. It's okay, I can do, she's strong, your – *como se dice* – your daughter?

ROSA. Yes. Daughter. *Mija.*

LYDIA. You go change, I take care here. *Hola-hola, chica.* What is her name?

ROSA. Ceci.

LYDIA. *Hola, Ceci. Hola.* I am Lydia. How are you? Fine? I am fine too. *Que bonita te ves con la avena en la cara.* Oatmeal is very good for the skin. Here.

*(She rubs more into her face. **CECI** freezes at the feel of the warm oatmeal. **ROSA** is taken aback.)*

Soon you be Miss *Tejas, que no*? Soon you be Miss *Universo.*

(**MISHA** *enters as* **CECI** *coos softly throughout the next passage.)*

MISHA. What's going on?

CECI. nnnnn…nnnnn…

ROSA. This is our maid –

LYDIA. Lydia.

ROSA. Lydia from Jalisco.

MISHA. What's she doing to her?

ROSA. She spilled the oatmeal on me and –

LYDIA. Making her skin soft. If she won't eat, then she can be beautiful. *¿Verdad, Ceci?*

CECI. Ooooh.

ROSA. I have to go change. I'm going to be late. I'm late already.

(**ROSA** *goes.)*

LYDIA. *Asi, asi.* Feels good, no? Feels like *chocolate.*

CECI. Gggnnh.

MISHA. Are you sure this works?

LYDIA. It worked on me, *que no*?

(She looks up at **MISHA** *for the first time.)*

What is your name?

MISHA. Miguel. But they call me Misha.

LYDIA. Misha?

MISHA. My mother's called me that since I was little.

LYDIA. It's Russian.

MISHA. I know.

LYDIA. Is there Russian in your blood?

MISHA. No. Listen, I think you really should get her cleaned up before my old man sees her like this. He's not into beauty tips n'shit –

LYDIA. Speak slower. Or speak Spanish.

MISHA. I'm not that fluent in Spanish.

LYDIA. Then speak slower, Misha.

MISHA. My. Father. Will be pissed. When he sees this. Pissed as in pissed off.

LYDIA. Ceci, are you calm now? You want to clean up and eat?

CECI. Ggnnh. Ggnnhr.

MISHA. That means yes.

LYDIA. No, it means let me wear it for another minute. Are we sharing a room?

MISHA. What?

LYDIA. Me and Ceci, are we sharing a room?

MISHA. Yeah.

LYDIA. *Bueno. Asi va ser.*

MISHA. How old are you?

LYDIA. How old are you?

MISHA. No, this is a relevant question. You can't take care of my sister if you're as young as you look.

LYDIA. Speak slower.

MISHA. I said, You, Can't, Take, Care –

LYDIA. I am as young as I look.

MISHA. Mom!

(**ROSA** *enters wearing a new dress.*)

ROSA. Shhht! *¡Tranquilo!* Don't you know your father's still sleeping! That's another thing. My husband, *mi marido,* he works nights till 6 in the morning, then sleeps most of the day. You have to be very quiet.

MISHA. You can't be serious.

ROSA. I'm going to work. *Toma,* keys to the house. And here's my number at work. She eats only food that I've marked with her name in the fridge, *con su nombre,* okay? And she wears diapers, *pero* still she has to be changed. *Si tienes tiempo.* If you don't, I'll do it when I get home.

LYDIA. I do it.

MISHA. You're gonna leave her with her.

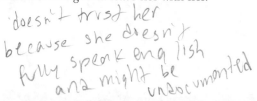

ROSA. My husband's name is Claudio and he keeps mostly to himself. Don't bother him. Stay away from Rene too, my oldest. This is Misha here, the only one who's not trouble.

LYDIA. I understand.

ROSA. The pay is thirty dollars a week and you'll be staying in Ceci's room at the end of the hall. *¿Que mas, que mas?* Oh, dinner is at six. I should be home right around that time. Okay?

LYDIA. Okay.

ROSA. *Gracias,* Lydia. Go to school and do your homework.

MISHA. Mom –

ROSA. *¡Que Dios te cuide, mijo!*

(She goes.)

CECI. Gghght.

LYDIA. Okay, now, she says.

MISHA. What?

LYDIA. Get the bath ready with some hot water.

MISHA. I have to go to school.

LYDIA. *Pues,* go. No problem. I'll do it.

MISHA. Besides, she had a bath yesterday.

LYDIA. She needs one today.

MISHA. Plus it might wake up my dad. You don't want to wake him when he's in a mood.

LYDIA. Speak slow –

MISHA. You don't want to wake my dad.

CECI. Ggngh, Gghn. Mmmgh.

LYDIA. *Bueno.* Bring to me a towel and some water.

*(**MISHA** goes.)*

CECI. Gghghnnnm.

LYDIA. It's not so good when it gets cold, ah? *Ay,* Ceci, you hold my hand so tight. *¿Que te pasa?* What do you want to tell me?

(**CECI** *guides her hand into her drawers.* **LYDIA** *discovers blood.)*

LYDIA. *(cont.)* Ah. *Sangrita.* It's your time, eh? Good. I will wash you very clean, *vas a ver.*

(**MISHA** *returns with a towel and a bowl of water.)*

Thank you.

(**LYDIA** *begins washing the oatmeal off* **CECI** *'s face.)*

MISHA. Why are you trying to speak English?

LYDIA. It's a beautiful *idioma.*

MISHA. But why do you want to learn it? You live in Jalisco.

LYDIA. I never say that. My friend, she is from Jalisco. I come from a *pueblo* outside of that. *En los montes.*

MISHA. We don't know anything about you.

LYDIA. You know my name. Are you going to school?

MISHA. What's it to you?

LYDIA. Because if no, help me with her. Hold her while I take off the wet clothes.

MISHA. What?

LYDIA. Help.

(He kneels by her as she pulls off **CECI** *'s pajamas.)*

MISHA. What do you want me to do?

LYDIA. Keep her not moving.

(She unbuttons her pajama top.)

MISHA. Wait.

LYDIA. *Andale,* Ceci.

MISHA. Wait.

CECI. Gggngnh.

(**LYDIA** *pulls off her top exposing* **CECI** *'s breasts.* **MISHA** *turns away.)*

MISHA. What are you doing! What the hell! I can't see her naked!

LYDIA. Why not?

MISHA. She's my sister! Jeez! Cover her. Please.

LYDIA. *¿Que onda?* You have not ever seen *chichis*?

(**CECI** *begins to laugh.*)

CECI. Gggngng-ghgnh-hhhah-hhgnhah.

LYDIA. Your brother.

MISHA. It's not right. I can't see her like this.

LYDIA. Then don't look.

(**LYDIA** *washes her quietly.* **MISHA** *slowly turns his gaze toward her.*)

Your sister has beautiful tits. But no-one to see them. Too bad.

(**MISHA** *is transfixed. Then his gaze meets* **CECI**'*s.*)

MISHA. When we were kids, at the church bazaar, she loved to play *Loteria.* There was this card called *La Sirena,* the Mermaid, and in the picture, her bare breasts rose above the water. It was her favorite card.

LYDIA. *¿Ves?* English is a pretty *idioma.* Write those pretty words down.

MISHA. I have to go.

(**MISHA** *gathers his books and rushes out.* **LYDIA** *fishes for a blouse from her own bag and puts it on* **CECI**.)

LYDIA. *Aver.* You will like this. *Mi abuelita* made it for me. The last time I wear, I was another girl. I sat before the *espejo* brushing my hair. Wondering: who is that looking back? Hm? Now let me see your room, *palomita.*

(*She takes up her bag and goes down the hall.* **CECI** *feels the fabric of this new blouse.*)

CECI. Now I remember. I'm horny! I'm just horny! I want to be wanted. I want to be touched. Not just touched, groped! I want to be fondled and strummed and tickled and…I want to be fucked. I want someone to plunge their hands into my body and grab that ball of fire burning my insides and hold it super tight till the *picante* bursts through my eyes! Ohhh! It feels so good but so BAD! How could you miss this, God? How could you take so much of my brain and still miss the part that craves the hokey pokey? Oh, who is this girl? What is she doing to me?

*(**LYDIA** returns in a plain dress and slippers. She has been cleaning the house. Broom and dust mop. She starts straightening up in the living room.)*

CECI. *(cont.)* Hours pass like seconds. She's fast as a bird's wing. Lydia the blur. She brings me soup but I don't remember slurping nothing but blur.

*(**CLAUDIO** enters, gruff and disoriented after a long daylight sleep. He stands in the middle of the room and stares at **LYDIA**, who stops and stares back.)*

LYDIA. Lydia. I am your maid. *(No reply.) ¿Cuantos años tiene su hija?*

CLAUDIO. *¿Hay café?*

LYDIA. In the kitchen. What happen to her? *(No reply.)* It's okay. She'll tell me.

(He glares at her then goes to the kitchen.)

Your father, he reminds me of someone. One of my *novios.* Always mad at something.

(He returns with a cup and turns on the stereo, puts on his headphones and sits to watch TV.)

I don't comprehend your coffee machine. If it is not good, I make again some more.

CECI. GGGhhnj.

LYDIA. If it's too strong, tell me. I like it strong, but for some peoples, coffee is not good that way.

CECI. Ggnnrhg.

LYDIA. He can't hear? Why not? I'm right here, he's right there.

CECI. Ggnhnh.

LYDIA. I see.

*(**LYDIA** dusts the TV, blocking his view. Then she dusts the stereo console. She finds the sleeve of the record album.)*

¡Ay, mira! ¡Pedro Infante! My mother's favorite!

(She raises the volume to full. **CLAUDIO** *rips off the headphones and jumps to his feet, his eyes glaring with rage.)*

CLAUDIO. HIJO DE LA CHINGADA!

LYDIA. How come she is like this.

CLAUDIO. *Un accidente. Chocó mi Pontiac.*

LYDIA. How long ago?

CLAUDIO. *Hace dos años.*

LYDIA. *¿Hace dos años?* Was it your fault?

CLAUDIO. *¿Que qué?*

LYDIA. You walk around like it's your fault. Did you crash the car with her inside?

CLAUDIO. *No.*

LYDIA. But you blame yourself.

CLAUDIO. *¿Que quieres de mi?*

LYDIA. Only this one thing: you like the coffee or not?

(He downs the cup in one gulp and throws it violently into the kitchen, shattering it.)

CLAUDIO. *No. No me gusta.*

(He goes back to his bedroom.)

LYDIA. *Pues*...I'll have to do better.

CECI. I...I see a new card, *El Pontiac Caliente*! The Pontiac in heat! Ceci in the Pontiac mad-crazy for some loco. Si, that ball of fire inside! Daddy's little girl in hip-hugger jeans, Red Keds, Carole King hair racing toward her miracle boy!

*(***LYDIA** *is cleaning up the mess as* **RENE** *comes in, sleepy.)*

RENE. What the hell was that?

LYDIA. I broke a cup.

RENE. Are you the maid?

LYDIA. Lydia. You are the other son.

RENE. Yeah. *¿Como the fuck esta?*

LYDIA. I…what?

RENE. Is she giving you any trouble?

LYDIA. Who, Ceci? No.

RENE. Slap her upside the head if she gets out of line. Kidding! Is there *café, por favor*?

LYDIA. *Si, pero* it's not good.

RENE. What do you mean it's not good? Get me a cup.

*(**LYDIA** goes.)*

CECI. Ggghnn.

RENE. I said I was kidding. Jesus Christ.

*(He stops and looks at **CECI**.)*

Look. Every breath, every beat of my heart, every drop of my blood, is yours. You own me. So quit giving me that look or die.

*(**LYDIA** returns with a new cup of coffee.)*

LYDIA. Here for you.

RENE. Okay, if you're talking English on account of us trans-border Mexicans, spare me the condescension. Talk Spanish in this house if you want.

LYDIA. *Bueno, si quiere que hable en mi idioma materno, asi lo prefiero también, pero primeramente, me gustaría explicarle un poco de mis deseos en este país –* .

RENE. Look, if you want to speak English here, I'm not going to stop you. Spanish sounds kinda uppity coming from you, anyway.

LYDIA. Uppit – uppit…?

RENE. It means gimme the damn coffee.

(He takes it and sips as she watches him.)

LYDIA. You don't like?

RENE. Not bad.

LYDIA. You don't go to school?

RENE. I'm done with that shit. You know, the more I look at you, the better this coffee tastes.

LYDIA. I'm glad.

RENE. What do you think of us? You find us disgusting? I know how much you Mexicans hold us in contempt.

LYDIA. Contempt…

RENE. You hate us. You hate us for coming here, for deserting the homeland for a chunk of that goddamn American dream, whatever the fuck that is. We're you watered-down and a little more well-off. So, do you like what you see?

LYDIA. I always like what I see.

RENE. So you think you're going to hold out long?

LYDIA. In this job or this country?

RENE. Both.

LYDIA. I hope yes.

RENE. I hope so too. You're easy on the eyes and hard somewhere else.

LYDIA. Your mama said you were trouble.

RENE. Better keep your door locked at night.

LYDIA. But I don't think you're trouble.

RENE. Righteous.

LYDIA. Is your coffee good now?

RENE. Best I ever tasted.

(He finishes it up and throws the empty cup into the kitchen. He goes back to his room.)

LYDIA. *Mano…*what happen to the men in this house?

CECI. Ghgngg, gghn. Ggn…teeee.

*(**LYDIA** goes to her. She touches her scar.)*

LYDIA. *De acuerdo.*

*(She touches **CECI**'s scar with tenderness.)*

Love is a big hurt. Even for fathers and brothers.

*(**CECI** touches her chest. **LYDIA** is caught in a pang she hadn't acknowledged before.)*

Have we met before, *muñeca*?

(**LYDIA** *goes. Lights change around* **CECI**.)

CECI. Maybe. Maybe we fell in each other's wounds one night. Into each other's mirrors. Crossed paths in our *vuelos*, said wassup with you, and then took a nap in the afterlife. Spooning in the afterlife, you and me. Or maybe we just wish we were sisters.

(The TV audio plays a mélange of everything that was on during the early 70s: news, variety shows, sitcoms, etc. **CLAUDIO, ROSA, RENE,** *and* **MISHA** *slowly enter with their TV trays of food and sit to watch TV.* **CLAUDIO** *has his headphones on.* **CECI** *lies on her mattress.)*

RENE. This pollo ain't bad.

ROSA. It's good.

MISHA. Real good.

RENE. Come to think of it, we're all eating a little better lately.

ROSA. *Que*, you don't like my cooking, *sinverguenza*?

MISHA. Mom, she makes chicken *molé* from scratch. She uses spices and stuff we don't even know how to pronounce. She's got recipes the Aztecs used on the damn pyramids.

ROSA. *Entonces* I won't cook for you no more. *Ingratos.*

RENE. Hey, a-hole, speaking of Aztecs, where's my Abraxas album?

MISHA. Oh. I was gonna ask you. I borrowed it for inspiration. I'm writing some poems for English based on the songs in Santana's album.

RENE. *¡No mames, guey!* You took my album to school?

MISHA. What's wrong with that?

RENE. *Baboso.* I had something special in the sleeve of that album.

MISHA. What?

RENE. Something very very imported.

ROSA. *¿De que estas hablando, mijo?*

RENE. Just some special papers, Mom. I appreciate your interest in poetry and art, bro, but you get that effin' album back. And stay out of my effin' room, while you're at it.

MISHA. It's my effin' room too.

RENE. Then stay out of my TOP half of it.

MISHA. Okay, then anything that falls out of the top half of your room is MINE.

RENE. And anything I step on in the bottom half is BROKE.

ROSA. *¡YA! Ay,* Praise God, sometimes I wish I had my own headphones too.

RENE. *Oye. Mira.* The *jefe* hasn't touched his supper.

MISHA. Maybe it's too spicy.

ROSA. *Oye, Viejo. ¿No tienes hambre?*

*(**CLAUDIO** looks at her. He takes off the headphones.)*

CLAUDIO. *No. Tengo que ir temprano esta noche.*

(He shrugs and goes.)

ROSA. That's four nights in a row he's going to work early.

MISHA. I think the maid makes him nervous.

ROSA. So what do you think of her?

RENE. Besides her cooking and her perky little breasts?

ROSA. Which reminds me. I don't like the way you're looking at her. *Portate bien.* Misha? What do you think of her?

MISHA. She does all right with Ceci. She likes her, too.

ROSA. She does, doesn't she?

CECI. Gggghhhn. Ggnhnn.

ROSA. Lydia!

*(**LYDIA** enters from down the hall. She notices that **CLAUDIO** has not eaten his food.)*

LYDIA. *Señora.*

ROSA. Ceci needs her diaper changed.

LYDIA. *Si, señora.*

(She goes to **CECI** *and slowly brings her to her feet.)*

ROSA. So what are these *poemas* you're writing, *mijo*?

MISHA. Ah, they're nothing special. Just some verses.

RENE. What about, bro? Oppression and *la raza unida* and our Indian roots?

MISHA. No, not like that. My first one's called Ode to a *Chanate.*

ROSA. A grackle? You wrote a poem about those nasty black birds who mess on my car every morning??

*(***LYDIA** *goes off with* **CECI***.)*

MISHA. They're beautiful. They got these oil-slick wings and yellow eyes and their song is so complex.

(There is a light knock on the door.)

ROSA. *¡Chale!* More like a squeaky garage door, *mijo*! Don't write no poems about them *chanates*!

*(***ROSA** *opens the door and* **ALVARO** *comes in, dressed in a large overcoat.)*

ALVARO. *Tia!*

ROSA. Oh my god! Alvaro!

ALVARO. I know, huh? I hope I'm not bothering you at this hour.

ROSA. No, no, we just finished eating. Come on, you, say hello to your cousin!

MISHA. Hey Varo. What's up?

ALVARO. You're growing tall, kid.

MISHA. About effin' time, dude.

ALVARO. I know. It's just, *sabes*, I've been a little busy.

MISHA. Little busy being a damn hero! I saw your picture in the paper!

ALVARO. *Ay*, that was nothin'. Hey Rene.

ROSA. Varo, we're so proud of you! *(kisses him) Que lindo te ves!* Take off your coat, make yourself at home! *¡Andale!*

ALVARO. Thank you, *Tia.*

(**ALVARO** *takes off his coat and reveals his Border Patrol uniform underneath.)*

MISHA. *¡Vato!* You joined the Border Patrol?

ROSA. *¡Ay, dios mio, que barbaridad!*

ALVARO. I thought you should be the first to know, being family and all. I signed up about a month ago and they fast-tracked me right into service. What do you think?

ROSA. I don't know what to say, *sobrino*!

MISHA. Are you nuts? You can't join *la Migra*!

ALVARO. Relax, cuz, I had to do it. Money, *sabes.* It was this or temp work at Manpower.

MISHA. It still doesn't make sense, Varo. You're better than this, *ese.*

ALVARO. You guys don't know what I been through. I learned some deep lessons in-country about – .

(**LYDIA** *enters.)*

LYDIA. *Cielos…*

ROSA. Lydia! *¡Ven, ven!* Lydia's taking care of Ceci.

ALVARO. Oh, *mucho gusto.*

ROSA. *Oh,* she has her papers and everything. We made sure of that.

ALVARO. *Placer.*

LYDIA. You're the cousin. She told me about you.

ROSA. What? Oh, *Ceci* can't talk, silly! Alvaro, want to sit down and eat? Here, have this.

LYDIA. That's Don Claudio's.

ROSA. *No te apures.* He'll have a cheeseburger at work. *¡Andale, provecho!*

ALVARO. It sure looks good, *tia.*

ROSA. Just don't mess your uniform. It's so starched and clean, praise God! *(to* **LYDIA***)* Go bring her…

(**ALVARO** *digs into* **CLAUDIO***'s plate with relish as* **LYDIA** *goes.)*

RENE. Lessons like what?

ALVARO. Lessons about what matters. Lessons about the sacrifices our mothers and fathers made for us. We fight for that every day, *primo*. Every day we protect the blessings of this life.

MISHA. And that's why you took the job?

ALVARO. We got our own DMZ right here.

MISHA. You mean the border?

ALVARO. As soon as I get back, what happens? Some *mojado* steals my mother's car. I look at the neighbor-hood kids and they're all *marijuanos* now. Everywhere I turn, there's some out-of-work alien taking up space. It doesn't matter what all I've done over there, I still have to wait in line for a job with these illegals.

MISHA. Dude, our Dad was an illegal alien.

ALVARO. But he got his papers. He became a naturalized citizen using the proper channels, didn't he, *Tia*?

ROSA. Oh yes. Yes. *Claro que si.*

MISHA. So you don't have any second thoughts about doing this to *raza*?

ALVARO. Who would you rather, the *gringos*? We take care of our own *mierda*, excuse the language, *señora*.

RENE. Is that really why you came, Varo? To show us your new uniform?

ALVARO. There was a time, cuz, when I thought I knew who I was, and what I wanted, but I just needed to grow up.

RENE. Grow up?

ALVARO. I mean wake up to the real-real. Remember when we used to play like ants in this room? That was a child's dream, Rene. We think the dream carries us all the way, but I got different expectations now.

RENE. What do you expect?

ALVARO. To come back and start my life right. This war was the best thing that happened to me. It pulled me out of the dream.

RENE. It was more than a dream to some people.

ALVARO. Then some people better wake up.

CLAUDIO. *(calling from off) ¡Rosa! ¡Papel del baño!*

ROSA. *¡Ay! ¡Este Señor! ¡Que verguenza! ¡Espera!...*

*(**ROSA** gets a roll of toilet paper from the cabinets and goes off.)*

ALVARO. How you doing, little cuz?

MISHA. Not sure. It's hard to see that uniform in this house. But at the same time, you're family.

ALVARO. That's right.

RENE. Not one letter. Not one damn letter.

ALVARO. I was short on stamps.

*(**MISHA** senses something between them.)*

MISHA. I'm gonna help...uh...I'm gonna...

(He takes the plates from the trays and goes into the kitchen.)

ALVARO. Pos, you're lookin' good. I heard you been in some fights.

RENE. What the hell do you think you're doing here?

ALVARO. What do you think? I came to see Ceci.

RENE. Bullshit.

ALVARO. Is that bed for her? Is that where she's sleeping now?

RENE. You got some nerve. In that uniform, too.

ALVARO. Never in my dreams did I see myself in this. But it suits me, Rene. It really does. I'm gonna be good at this.

RENE. I bet you will.

ALVARO. How is she?

RENE. Now you ask. Now it occurs to you.

ALVARO. Look, man, what do you want from me? I'm here.

RENE. I wanna know where we stand.

ALVARO. We stand by the family, Rene. We stand by Ceci.

RENE. Why didn't you come sooner?

ALVARO. I couldn't.

RENE. But why? I'm talking to you!

ALVARO. 'Cause when I come near you, everything gets so confused. Things happen way too fast for me. You move at this crazy speed 'cause you're a blaze, *ese*, you don't give a shit. But I can't be selfish now. Look what happened.

RENE. She loved you, *ese.* She believed in you.

ALVARO. That's the problem. Everyone fucking believes in me.

RENE. Is that why you ran? Is that why you didn't even stay long enough to see how she was?

ALVARO. You eat shit. Don't forget where I been for the last two years. What I went through trumps anything you throw in my face. I've moved on. So don't lay your guilt at my feet.

RENE. She was crazy for you –

ALVARO. – Yeah? –

RENE. – She waited years for some word from you. A card. Anything.

ALVARO. How do you know? How the fuck do you know? If she can't talk, how do you know she missed me?

RENE. 'Cause I stayed, fucker! I stayed and took the heat for you!

ALVARO. Poor cuz. Still picking glass off your face....

(**ALVARO** *touches* **RENE**'*s lip.* **MISHA** *enters and* **RENE** *moves away.*)

MISHA. What's going on.

ALVARO. *Nada,* Meesh.

(**ROSA** *enters with a photo album.*)

ROSA. *Oye, sobrino. Mira.* She made a scrapbook of you. She glued all your pictures on it, Polaroids of you and her. See, your ribbons from track and wrestling.

ALVARO. Wow. I never realized.

ROSA. And the newspaper articles. When you were Homecoming King. And Student Council *y todo.* And look all your notes to her. And the songs she copied from the Hit Parade.

ALVARO. All of this for me.

ROSA. She had a big crush on you, *sobrino.* She woulda been so proud of your service.

MISHA. Mom, she ain't dead.

(**CLAUDIO** *enters dressed in his whites. He sizes* **ALVARO** *up with a scowl.)*

ALVARO. *Buenas, Tio.*

CLAUDIO. *Sobrino. ¿Y tu Abuela Doña Yolie?*

ALVARO. *Bien, gracias. Tio,* I'm in the *Migración.*

CLAUDIO. Good. Keep them all out.

(He grabs his coat and walks out past them.)

ROSA. Well. That was easy.

ALVARO. *Pues,* I better get going too.

ROSA. But you haven't seen Cecilia! –

ALVARO. Another day, *Tia.* I go on duty in fifteen minutes. I'm on the levee just up the road. Look, if you guys decide to hate me for this, I'll understand.

ROSA. *(kissing him on the cheek)* I'm going to pray for you. I'm going to ask Jesus to make these *mojaditos* lay their souls before your badge and give up without a struggle so no-one gets hurt.

ALVARO. *Gracias, Tia Rosa.*

CECI. Ggghfnaaaalgg.

(**MISHA** *is the first to see* **LYDIA** *ushering* **CECI** *into the room in her quinceañera dress and shoes and her hair pinned up. Everyone is stunned.)*

MISHA. Oh my god.

ALVARO. Ceci.

RENE. What do you think you're doing?

LYDIA. She wanted to wear this. She said Alvaro would have the first dance. In her *quinceañera.* First her dad, then you. Because you know her better than anyone.

ALVARO. Jesus.

ROSA. Lydia, *por favor* –

LYDIA. *A bailar, caballero.*

*(**ALVARO** goes to **CECI** and takes her hands. He carefully lifts her up and dances gently around the room with her. Everyone watches except **RENE** who looks away. "Sabor a Mi" plays in **CECI**'s mind.)*

CECI. Lydia, in your world the things that never happen always happen. With him. All my urges saved for him. Catching moonlight on the folds of my gown. A big corsage aflame on my heart. My pearl earrings on, dancing super-slow with Varo in the middle of the *salón* to *Sabor a mi*, body to body, cheek to cheek, his breath in my ear saying over and over –

ALVARO. Ceci…Ceci…Ceci –

*(She grasps **ALVARO** around the neck as if to hold him forever.)*

RENE. Ceci, let him go.

MISHA. Leave them alone.

LYDIA. Let her dance.

RENE. Ceci! I mean it!

*(A small wet spot gathers around **CECI** as she pees herself.)*

CECI. Gghgngg.

ROSA. *¡Ay dios mio! ¡Que desastre! ¡Mira nomas!* She's doing number one!

ALVARO. Ceci…please…my uniform…

RENE. CECI GODDAMMIT STUPID BITCH!

ROSA. RENE! NO!!

*(**RENE** tears **CECI** away from **ALVARO** and she collapses in a heap crying aloud.)*

MISHA. See what you done? Look at her! Are you happy? Is this what you wanted? You asshole!

*(**LYDIA** rushes to **CECI**.)*

ALVARO. I have to go.

ROSA. *¡Perdon, sobrino!* We're so sorry about this! I wish you didn't –

ALVARO. No, I'm sorry! Thank you for the good food. I have to go!

(**ALVARO** *rushes out.* **MISHA** *and* **LYDIA** *console* **CECI** *as she cries.)*

MISHA. It's okay, sis. It's over now. *(to* **RENE***)* You didn't have to be so rough with her.

RENE. I didn't put her in that dress.

MISHA. Still, you didn't have to push her away like that, fuckhead! What's your problem!

RENE. My problem is this maid doesn't realize what that fucking dress means in this house!

LYDIA. But she does.

RENE. Who asked you to talk?

LYDIA. She knows everyone's pain. All the time. Even yours.

RENE. Did she really ask you to put her in this dress?

LYDIA. How else would I know where to look?

ROSA. She told you?

RENE. Did she also tell you how she got her head stitched up like a baseball? Did she say who did that to her?

LYDIA. Not everything she says comes out her mouth.

RENE. What's that supposed to mean? What are these riddles? Who the fuck are you?

ROSA. *¡No hables asi, Rene!*

RENE. No! Explain to me! How do you know what she wants? As far as we can tell, the best she can do is nod when she needs to take a shit!

LYDIA. She loves you, Rene. She thinks you should be what you are, and not be sorry for it.

RENE. What??

(The sound of a car pulling up.)

MISHA. Dad.

ROSA. *(eyes landing on his wallet) ¡Dios mio!* He's coming back. Take her to bathroom! Get the dress off *de volada*!

LYDIA. Why?

RENE. You screwed yourself this time, maid.

MISHA. He's coming!

ROSA. *¡Andale! (seeing his wallet) Ay, la cartera!* His wallet!

(**CLAUDIO** *enters. He takes his wallet. He sees* **CECI** *in her dress.)*

CLAUDIO. *¿Quien hiso esto?*

ROSA. *Mira,* Claudio, it's not a big –

CLAUDIO. *¿Quien le puso esta chingadera a mija?*

CECI. Ggghgh.

CLAUDIO. *¿QUE QUIEN LO HISO?*

(**MISHA** *steps forward.)*

MISHA. Me. I did it.

(**CLAUDIO** *looks at* **CECI** *and shakes his head.)*

I just thought it was time, Dad. She looks so…divine. *¿No se te parece divina, Apa?*

(**CLAUDIO** *charges with flying fists at* **MISHA** *who collapses under the thrust.)*

CLAUDIO. *¡Cabron! ¡Te voy a matar, maldito!*

ROSA. *¡Ay, Viejo! NO! NO!*

(He pommels **MISHA. LYDIA** *screams as* **ROSA** *tries to intercede.* **RENE** *turns his back to them.)*

ROSA. *¡Dejalo! ¡No le peges!*

(**CLAUDIO** *blindly socks* **ROSA** *as he throws* **MISHA** *down the hall and follows him out, taking off his belt. The door slams. Everyone hears the lashes and* **MISHA***'s cries in the house.)*

Ya no le peges, Viejo, please *Diosito Santo,* make him stop, please not Misha, ayyy…ayyy…

(**LYDIA** *glares at* **RENE,** *who watches helplessly then runs out of the house. The lashes continue as the lights change.)*

CECI. New card. *La Mierda.* The Shit. This thing lashing me, this burning need to hurt, *carnal mayor,* you tore me away from him, my bronze star, how come! How come! And what's this thing that blackens my *corazón* when it's Varo my body craves?

*(**ROSA** enters, a shiner developing on her eye. She puts on her coat and gets her keys.)*

LYDIA. Are you sure you should be going, *señora*?

ROSA. I have to go look for him. Rene is very sensitive. He acts tough, but inside he's scared.

LYDIA. Of what?

ROSA. His father. Himself. Everything. He won't even drive a car since Ceci's accident. Lord, take care of my boy!

LYDIA. Where are you going to look?

ROSA. I'll drive around till I see him. He can't be far. Misha's sleeping now. He just needs some rest.

LYDIA. We should take him to the hospital.

ROSA. No, no, they ask too many questions. He'll be okay in the morning.

LYDIA. *Lo dudo, Señora. Se me parece muy malo.* And your eye too.

ROSA. Please, Lydia. It's happened before. He'll be all right. Stay here with Ceci.

*(**ROSA** goes. **LYDIA** sits by on the sofa and places her hand on her chest.)*

CECI. In your world, Lydia, people die and come back but not all the way. Not all the way.

*(**MISHA** comes into the living room. Swollen and blue with pounding. A cut above his eye.)*

MISHA. Mom? Mom?

*(**CECI** sees him and whines in alarm for him.)*

CECI. Eeeeeey. Eeeeey.

MISHA. Shh. It's okay, girl. I'm all right. See? Just a little puffy.

LYDIA. You should be lying down. Go lie down.

MISHA. Where's Mom? Is she okay?

LYDIA. She's looking for Rene. Sit. I'll get some more ice.

(**MISHA** *sits while* **LYDIA** *goes to the kitchen.)*

MISHA. You know what, Ceci? He's getting old. He can't keep pace anymore. Still, when he's mad, he can land some real-life hurt.

(**LYDIA** *returns with some ice in a dishcloth.)*

LYDIA. He was an animal. Only an animal does this.

MISHA. Didn't you earn your whippings growing up?

LYDIA. *Nunca.*

MISHA. In this town, it's a rite of passage.

LYDIA. Why did you do that? Why did you take blame for the *vestido*?

MISHA. I wasn't gonna let him work you over.

LYDIA. He would not.

MISHA. You don't know my dad.

LYDIA. You don't know me.

MISHA. Besides, you made her beautiful. I didn't believe she could be like that and still look so beautiful.

LYDIA. She is.

MISHA. You can't leave now. Ceci needs you.

(**LYDIA** *pops him with the ice on his face.)*

Ow.

LYDIA. Sorry.

MISHA. So what do *you* do for kicks in your hometown?

LYDIA. Town? More like a *campo santo.* Barren fields and empty houses. A lot of people gone to *El Norte.* We go to school. In the afternoons, we help our *mamas* with the chores. I'm an orphan so mostly I took care of my *abuela.*

MISHA. Did you have a…a *novio*?

LYDIA. Once. But he was too possessive. Then my grandmother died. I needed something to do.

MISHA. What do you want to do?

LYDIA. Learn English. Work in a hospital. I could be a good nurse.

MISHA. Yeah, but you need skills for that. Owww! My back's on fire.

LYDIA. Take off your shirt. *(He gives her a look.) ¡Ay, por favor!* Let me see your back!

(He takes off his shirt. His back is covered with raised welts, some of them bleeding.)

LYDIA. *O Señor.* Wait here.

(She runs down the hall to her room.)

CECI. Ggghgngn.

MISHA. Hey, it's only fair, I saw *you* topless.

CECI. Ggnn. Llglnh.

MISHA. You loved him, didn't you?

CECI. What sucks is that I still do. His thorns are all around my heart.

*(**LYDIA** returns with a small vial and a lit candle.)*

LYDIA. *Aver.*

MISHA. What's that?

LYDIA. I have skills. I learned them from my grandmother.

MISHA. Ahh. What is that stuff?

LYDIA. It's some liniment made from the *agave.* We use it to heal open wounds.

MISHA. Well, it's not working.

LYDIA. Of course not. You need to seal with this.

(She drips hot wax on his back.)

MISHA. OOOWW! OWWW! What are you doing to me! That burns!

LYDIA. You'll start to feel better now.

MISHA. What is this, some kinda witchcraft?

LYDIA. *Mi abuela* was a *curandera.* I learned the science of herbs growing up with her in her *botica.*

MISHA. Well, your science burns like shit.

LYDIA. Get your mind off it. Tell me this poem of the grackle.

MISHA. What?

LYDIA. You said you had a poem. How does it go?

MISHA. Well…

LYDIA. You don't know it from memory?

MISHA. I do.

LYDIA. *¿Entonces?* Don't be shy. What's it called.

MISHA. Ode to a *Chanate.* Ode means –

LYDIA. *Oda*, I know. *Dale.*

MISHA. O bird
You black bird
You look like you flew through the darkest night and it stuck on you,
Except you closed your eyes and they stayed yellow
As the wasps that dance around the lawn.
I see you sitting on the wire
Making that song, that grackle, crackle, wheeze, and chirp
That makes me wonder if you're trying to learn
the language of manual transmissions
Or maybe you're trying to say something in our broken tongue.
O bird dressed in mourning but always so lively,
Like death is just another occasion to find a she-grackle,
You remind me of things I should be doing,
Flights I should be taking, nights I should be soaking my wings in.
Except with eyes opened 'cause mine are already black.

Well?

LYDIA. The transmission part. I didn't get that.

MISHA. It's a draft. I'm still working on it. Hey. I don't feel it anymore.

LYDIA. Put your shirt on. Your poem is good. But to know words, you have to know people. Not grackles.

*(**ROSA** enters and finds **MISHA** without his shirt on.)*

ROSA. *¿Que es esto?*

MISHA. I was…I'm tired. I have to go to bed.

(He goes.)

LYDIA. *Señora –*

ROSA. I found him.

*(**RENE** enters, morose and withdrawn. He looks like a child.)*

LYDIA. Rene?

ROSA. Don't talk to him. Go to bed, *mijo.*

*(She kisses him and he starts to go, eyes to the floor. He stops and falls before **CECI**.)*

RENE. Sorrysorrysorrysorrysorrysorrysorrysorryi'msorryi'm sorrycecii'msosorry.

(He gets up and goes down the hall to his room.)

ROSA. You too. Go sleep. I'm tired. I have to work tomorrow. *(feeling her puffy eye)* How will I explain this?

LYDIA. She wanted to wear the dress. She told me so.

ROSA. I understand. But leave the miracles to God.

*(**LYDIA** goes. **ROSA** casts a glance toward **CECI**.)*

You know where I found him, don't you?

*(**ROSA** goes.)*

CECI. Where hearts and Pontiacs break. It's all love, *Ama.* All a desperate *abrazo.* All of us holding tight to each other so we don't fall so hard. So we can open our eyes again and see the new sun dripping in through the blinds.

*(The following dawn. **CLAUDIO** comes in. His whites stained with grease and ketchup. He finds **CECI** sleeping, still wearing the dress.)*

CLAUDIO. *Mi pajarita. Como te quiero.* 'Cause of you I given up.

(**LYDIA** *enters in her clothes with her bag.)*

LYDIA. *Ya me voy.*

CLAUDIO. *¿A donde?*

LYDIA. *¿Que te importa?*. You beat him very badly. Your own son.

CLAUDIO. *¡Pero mira como la vistio!*

LYDIA. It was me, stupid. I dressed her in it. You going to beat me too?

CLAUDIO. *Espera.*

(She stops. **CLAUDIO** *struggles to frame his words.)*

Era mi pajarita…

LYDIA. In English. You want me to listen, tell me in English.

CLAUDIO. Cecilia…my bird. Why you put the dress?

LYDIA. It's her dress. She wanted to look nice for…for you.

CLAUDIO. It's good you go back. This country rob your soul.

LYDIA. Hombre, you have a life here.

CLAUDIO. I had a life *aya! Pero* the way you want things and the way things go: different. Rosa want her babies *que sean Americanos.* So here I am, not one, not the other, but a, *como se dice,* a stone. A stone for them to make their own great *pinche* dreams.

CECI. Ggngnnh.

LYDIA. Except Cecilia.

CLAUDIO. You want to know *que paso,* for reals?

LYDIA. No.

CECI. Yes.

CLAUDIO. Three days till *la quinceañera.* Three days. Dinner set, salon reserve, the *comadres* all prepare. But *en medio de la noche,* everyones sleeping and me at work, *Ceci y Rene* out the window, and nobody hears *nada.* Why?

CECI. 'Cause this is the night: the night of secrets: of dark streets and Pontiacs and fires in my body.

CLAUDIO. Why push it the car in neutral down the street and then start it up? Why?

CECI. 'Cause a fierce voice in our hearts is hissing *Vamonos!*

CLAUDIO. *Con las alas del diablo* they tear down to the border *en el* West Side! Why!

CECI. There is no why! Fuck all the whys! Only me and Rene and the roar of the car!

CLAUDIO. Three nights till the *quinceañera y se van,* they go somewhere too fast, *los pendejos* –

CECI. To Alvaro! Alvaro my love! I'm coming!

CLAUDIO. Too fast down *ese* dirt road by the Border fence, and the tires are bald *en ese* Pontiac, you can't drive too fast in that car! Then something happen –

CECI. This ugliness. This hot ugly bile inside rolling up my throat!

CLAUDIO. Rene's good, he drive good. But something make him miss the big curve, you have to slow down to turn, but Rene, he don't slow, he don't turn and – !

CECI. NO!

CLAUDIO. The car hit a pole *y ya.*

CECI. *El Pontiac* wrapped around a pole like a lover and me flying in a sky full of confetti glass

CLAUDIO. *Mi* Cecilia, who is born on a full moon and dance the twist for me at six, who always understand me no matter what demon possess me. Cecilia Rosario Flores, her name on the cake of her fifteen year, fly through the windshield of the car into the cold hard ground fifty feet *en frente.*

CECI. I see little bits of brain and blood on the road, and you trying to scoop up all the memories, my first words, my first dreams, you try to scoop them up in your hands, *Apa.*

LYDIA. And Rene.

CLAUDIO. *Nada.* I ask him why. I ask him where the *chingados* they go. A million whys I ask him. He sit in the dirt and cry. He never answer, never.

LYDIA. You still blame him, don't you?

CLAUDIO. Blame is not the word. I wish you peace of mind wherever you go.

(He puts on his headphones and stares at the blank TV.)

LYDIA. Peace of mind. What is that.

(About to leave, **LYDIA** *catches* **CECI***'s gaze. A kind of plea in her look.)*

CECI. I had a dream the night before you came. That you stand at the door and stop breathing. And a part of you falls away…

*(***LYDIA** *sets her bag down and peels off her underwear. She approaches* **CLAUDIO** *who stares straight at the TV.)*

That you come like a ghost into our house and stand over my daddy, who's a ghost himself, and you take his crown and hear the voices in his heart crying for love…

(She takes off his headphones. She places them over her head and listens for a moment.)

And then you blind him…

(She turns off the TV. He remains still with his eyes fixed ahead.)

And land on his lap and take his breath away.

(She straddles him in his chair and kisses him. He enfolds her in his arms and begins to cry.)

Each breathless *beso* reaches into his heart and lays grout over the crumbling walls of his pride, you touch him who can't remember *touch* any more than I can. It was a dream more real than this maid on my father making sex like the last act of God, I see your eyes, Lydia, dreaming the same thing, burning their grief into me, their want, their reckless need for darkness –

(She turns and meets **LYDIA***'s gaze.)*

I see — you! With the inscription La Muerte, La Muerte, La Muerrr…

(They continue to make love as **CECI** *goes into convulsions.)*

gngghgnghg.gfhghgngng.

(Out of the shadows, **RENE** *watches them making love as music from the headphones plays.)*

(curtain)

End Of Act 1

ACT 2

(The living room in **CECI***'s dream. Bedsheets stretched everywhere over chairs and tables, creating a network of glowing tunnels amid the darkness.* **CECI** *wearing the quinceañera dress crawls on all fours like a toddler through the tunnels.)*

CECI. Teeteetee. Teeteetee. Teetee means home. Teeteetee. Queen ant Ceci looks for a nest for her *huevitos.* Teeteetee in ant-language means SOON!

*(***MISHA***'s shadow appears crawling along a bedsheet.)*

MISHA. Teeteeteeteeeeeee!

CECI. Teetee! That's Ant for over here, Misha! Teeteetee!

*(***MISHA** *appears with a naked G.I. Joe in his mouth.)*

MISHA/CECI. Teeteeteeteeteeetee!

CECI. What's this, worker ant?

MISHA. I bring you food, Queen.

CECI. This is not the stuffed mouse.

MISHA. I couldn't find the stuffed mouse.

CECI. Well, this doll doesn't cut it.

MISHA. It's not a doll!

CECI. Ugh. It's got spit all over.

MISHA. Can we play?

CECI. Teeteeteeeee! That means how do you like my egg-laying chamber?

MISHA. Teeteetee means bitchin'. How many eggs?

CECI. I am a shy queen, so I can't tell you. But antenna to antenna you can read my mind.

(They place their fingers on their heads and touch "antennae.")

CECI/MISHA. Teee-teeeeeee-teeeeee.

(More shadows appear on the suspended sheets. **RENE** *and* **ALVARO** *crawl through a portal.)*

RENE. Tee-tee-teeee.

ALVARO. Tee-tee-teeee.

ALL. Tee-teee-teeeee.

CECI. Soldier ants! Defenders of the colony! Teetee means welcome!

RENE. *Mi reina,* we got great news. We defeated the evil anteater and stripped the flesh from his *huesos.*

ALVARO. And we attacked the boy who stepped on our anthill. We stung him right on the teetees!

CECI. Then let the ant-revels begin.

(They crawl in frantic circles shaking their heads at each other.)

ALL. TEE-TEE-TEE-TEE-TEE-TEEE!

*(***MISHA, RENE,** *and* **ALVARO** *slip into the maelstrom of sheets, casting shadows on the walls.)*

CECI. Tee-tee means I love my ants. I love all my little ants crawling through *La Vida Cecilia,* memories of innocence, tee-tee, *ormigas* forever, in ant-language there's no word for die. Teeee.

(The shadows of **ALVARO** *and* **RENE** *first touch antennae and then kiss, long and gently.)*

I see behind the sheets secret ant-affection in the tunnels of our *corazones,* cousins and *carnales,* finding their hearts in each others' mouths.

(The shadows vanish and **LYDIA** *appears gathering the sheets into her laundry basket.* **LYDIA** *looks smart in* **CECI***'s jeans and blouse.)*

In ant-language, there *is* a word for live and it's Lydia. I saw the love going dark in your eyes and it means *we* ain't lived enough yet, we ain't died enough yet…we ain't…Lydhghghg….

(Lights up on the house. It's cleaner. **CECI** *is in* **CLAUDIO***'s chair, staring at the TV.* **ROSA, RENE** *and* **LYDIA** *work at the coffee table on stamp books, with the laundry basket beside* **LYDIA. MISHA** *sits by* **CECI** *writing on a legal pad.)*

ROSA. She's quiet.

MISHA. Saturdays. Space Ghost and Scooby Doo.

ROSA. *O si. Los monitos.*

LYDIA. Tell me again, *Señora,* how does this work? I don't get it.

ROSA. *Primero,* you get these stamps from the Piggly-Wiggly when you shop and you put them away in the kitchen cabinet till you get a *monton* of them. Then you stick them on these S&H saver books. All of these pages you fill, *ves?* Then when you get enough *libritos* filled, you go to the catalogue and pick out the things you want, go to the S&H store and trade the books for them.

LYDIA. *¿Gratis?*

ROSA. *Free!*

RENE. It's all crap, though.

ROSA. Oh, *si,* Mr. Smarty-*calzones*? What about that umbrella stand I got last time?

RENE. We don't have any umbrellas.

MISHA. Plus it never rains here.

ROSA. And that casserole dish? That was nice, *verdad*!

RENE. You've never made a casserole in your life. You use it for the *chile.*

ROSA. And that little shelf for the family pictures? That cost me 10 books!

RENE. I saw that at the Winn's Five and Dime for three dollars!

ROSA. *¡Ay, si tu!* Quit talking and keep licking!

*(***CLAUDIO** *emerges from his room and walks through on his way to the kitchen, upstage.)*

Did we wake you? We were trying to be quiet.

CLAUDIO. I couldn't sleep. *¿Hay café?*

LYDIA. Fresh pot the way you like.

CLAUDIO. *(realizing that she is in* **CECI** *'s clothes) ¿Que es eso?*

LYDIA. Oh, some clothes *Señora* gave me.

ROSA. Just some old things *de* Ceci's. She fits into them perfect, *que no?*

LYDIA. *¿Le gusta, señor?*

(He regards her with a mixture of scorn and misgiving. Then goes into the kitchen.)

Maybe I should change.

ROSA. No, no, Lydia, he likes it! You look more like us, more American.

MISHA. More like Ceci.

RENE. That must trip the old man out.

LYDIA. I have to do the wash now.

ROSA. Misha, come take her place and help us lick the stamps.

MISHA. I'm busy.

ROSA. Busy-*ni-que*-busy! What are you doing!

RENE. Writin' poems, what else.

ROSA. Not about those *chanates*, I hope!

RENE. No, he's writing love poems for –

MISHA. Shuttup.

*(***MISHA** *puts his pad aside and goes to the stamp books as* **CLAUDIO** *calls for* **LYDIA**, *who glowers at* **RENE**.*)*

CLAUDIO. *(in the kitchen)* Lydia!

LYDIA. You're a bad one.

RENE. What?

*(***LYDIA** *goes into the kitchen.)*

ROSA. *¿De que hablan?* What's going on here?

MISHA. Nothin', Mom.

ROSA. *Mira,* nothing gets past me. I see everything in this house.

RENE. Right.

ROSA. And what I don't see, the Lord does.

RENE. I bet he's enjoying the show. Right, bro?

(He licks his stamps in a lewd way when **MISHA** *looks.)*

CECI. I smell it. My dad and Lydia's combustion. Lydia sprayed some Glade, but I catch that whiff of sweat and bygone dreams. Like an invisible *piñata* full of stale candies.

(In the kitchen, **LYDIA** *and* **CLAUDIO** *hover uneasily over the coffee.)*

CLAUDIO. *¿Que estas pensando con esta – ?*

LYDIA. English.

CECI. Nobody but me hears what they're saying in the kitchen.

CLAUDIO. Will you come to me again?

CECI. The longing in their voices…

LYDIA. No.

CECI. Not for each other, but for other things out of their conception. Things that require light and mindless hurt…

MISHA. What are you redeeming this time, Mom?

ROSA. This set of knives, *mira.* These are special Cheff's knives, very high quality, five of them, *imaginate.* I always wanted a set.

MISHA. It's pronounced Shef, Mom. The French way.

ROSA. *Pues,* when I go to France, *asi lo digo.* Here I say Cheff. How are you feeling?

MISHA. Mom, it's been a week. I'm fine.

*(***LYDIA** *passes through with the wash.)*

ROSA. He didn't mean to hit you like that, you know. He was expecting me to stop him. I just didn't know how. It was my fault.

MISHA. It was nobody's fault, okay?

*(***CLAUDIO** *walks through on his way to the bedroom. Silence.)*

ROSA. *(going through her purse)* Anyways. After work I stopped at Mr. Dickey's Jewlery Store and…

(She gives him a small case.)

MISHA. Mom...

(He opens it.)

ROSA. It's a Cross. A gold Cross pen.

RENE. *Vato.* Cool.

MISHA. *(taking the gold pen out)* Mom, are you sure about this? These pens are expensive.

ROSA. I'm working, Misha. We're quasi-middle class as of today, which means we live a little *mas* better. Besides, it was on clearance, half off. I always wait for the half-off sales.

MISHA. Thanks, Mom. Feel this, Rene. Feel how heavy it is.

RENE. That's heavy.

MISHA. Words. Full of words, *carnal.*

ROSA. Just no bad words, okay? I hate when you write bad words.

MISHA. If I use them, Mom, I promise you won't know what they mean.

ROSA. Misha, you're going to be somebody. Even if you won't have God, God's grace is on you.

(She goes, wiping her eyes.)

MISHA. What's with her? She's all goofy lately.

RENE. Leave her alone. She's doing her best.

MISHA. Her best to what?

RENE. Dude, you're so damned naïve. You got no idea how fucked up we are.

MISHA. I'm not as naïve as you think I am.

RENE. *(grabbing his pad)* Oh yeah? What's this, fuckhead?

MISHA. Don't touch that. Put it down.

RENE. "Black eyes drenched in the waters of the Rio"

MISHA. Give it!

RENE. "Black hair like a mantilla draped on me."

MISHA. I told you –

RENE. "Your brown hands rolling over the open plain of my back."

MISHA. Asshole.

RENE. I gotta say, Misha, I never seen you like this. It seems our little housekeeper from Mexico-way has sparked your plumed serpent to life, *carnal. (tossing his pad back)* Too bad it's wasted.

MISHA. What do you know?… Has she told you anything?

RENE. *¡No mames!* Seriously, in the interest of family pride and the welfare of my little brother who truly understands shit about affairs of the *pinchi* heart, I gotta say this: get over this fucking bitch as quick as you can.

MISHA. What?

RENE. She's a whore, Miguel. You're writing love poems to a low-class Mexican whore. Come on, *ese,* she's the maid. Don't you know it's a taboo? Haven't you been watching the *novelas*?

MISHA. Fuck you. I'm not listening to this.

RENE. I'm just watching out for you, *ese.*

MISHA. Like you watched me get creamed by Dad last week? Like you came to my defense then?

RENE. That's different.

MISHA. How is that different?

RENE. I wanted to help.

MISHA. Then why didn't you?

RENE. It wasn't possible.

MISHA. What kind of fucked-up answer is that?

RENE. It wasn't possible, okay? I got my own ways of getting back at the old man.

MISHA. What good does that do me? Finally you're big enough to take him on. You can make it stop any time. Either you're a goddamn coward or you want him to kill me.

RENE. I'd drop this if I were you.

MISHA. Listen, do me a favor and go back to beating up defenseless homos like you actually do. We prefer reality here.

RENE. You're out of line, Miguel.

MISHA. C'mon, who are you fooling? It's not *gangas* and Ft. Bliss GI's you been jumpin'. Everyone knows it's just the local homos.

RENE. Where do you get this crap?

MISHA. Serge told his kid brother and he came and told me. You go to all the same places they go, the same strips, the same cruising spots, the word's out, man.

RENE. What are you saying?

MISHA. You're a fag-basher, you and your buddies. It's sick, it's pathetic, bro, and it's only a matter of time before this shit catches up with you.

RENE. What shit! Tell me, what shit is catching up with me!

MISHA. Lemme ask you: whose fuckin' ass do you really wanna kick! Ask yourself. Who you really wanna hurt!

RENE. *¡No mames, guey*! You don't know Thing One about this.

MISHA. It's been two years, carnal. When are you gonna get over it? When are you gonna stop making everyone pay for that crash?

RENE. Keep your maid away from me. If you want her, fine, let her be your damned –

MISHA. Don't you say it. Don't say that word to my face.

RENE. Whore.

(**LYDIA** *comes in with a pair of scissors. They all stand looking at each other.)*

CECI. These cartoons, amazin' how they go through so much hell, but nobody ever gets hurt. Just little bronze *estrellitas* over their heads and these magic bandages that vanish in the next frame. That's why they don't have private parts. They'll be safe as long as they don't screw each other blind.

*(**RENE** falters under **LYDIA**'s stare and stalks out the door. **MISHA** gathers the saver books and puts them all in a bag. **LYDIA** starts cutting the plastic covers off the lampshades. **ROSA** enters.)*

ROSA. What are you doing?

LYDIA. *Señora,* I saw the pictures in that catalogue. Lampshades like yours.

ROSA. Yes?

LYDIA. Except they don't have the *plastico* on them. It's just how they were…*como se dice….*

MISHA. Packaged.

ROSA. But it keeps the dust off them.

MISHA. Mom, she's right. You're supposed to take them off when you put them up.

ROSA. But we've had them like this forever.

LYDIA. Well, it's all wrong. That's why the light is so bad in this house.

ROSA. Then why didn't you say something? Why didn't none of you say something?

MISHA. We didn't want to embarrass you.

LYDIA. See? Don't they look *mas* better?

ROSA. *Pues…*

LYDIA. Now you can see things.

ROSA. Next time, ask me, Lydia.

LYDIA. I thought I –

ROSA. *(snapping at her angrily)* You didn't. Ask me before you start redoing my house!

LYDIA. *Mi culpa, Señora.* I didn't mean to be so *presumida.*

*(**ROSA** glowers at her for a moment.)*

CECI. Mggn. Nggnh.

MISHA. Look, Mom, Ceci likes it too.

*(**ROSA** looks uneasily at **CECI**, then at **LYDIA**, then at the lights in the room.)*

ROSA. *Ay, como soy tonta.* You're right. It does look brighter. *(laughing nervously)* I can be so dumb sometimes! Such a *ranchera!*

LYDIA. *Señora Rosa,* don't talk like that. You're good people. You been nicer than my own mother to me. I'm sorry.

ROSA. Thank you, *mija....* *(touches her face)* You know what? Let me take you shopping. *¡Andale, vamonos* shopping*!*

LYDIA. *¿Que qué?*

ROSA. Come with me! I hate going to the stores alone! *Además,* I'm going to need help with the bags.

LYDIA. *O señora,* there's work to do....

ROSA. *Chale,* the work can wait. Besides, you made Ceci happy. *Ven conmigo, mija.* Help me pick out some things for the house. *Pronto,* get your *chaqueta* and let's go!

LYDIA. *Señora,* you are too nice!

*(**LYDIA** runs off for her jacket.)*

ROSA. Misha, stay with your sister. We'll be back. *(darkening in a flash)* And next time, you let me know about things like this, *me oyes?*

MISHA. Okay.

ROSA. *Vamos, mija.*

*(She takes her keys and goes out. **LYDIA** enters with her jacket and starts to go out the door, but stops when she sees **MISHA** writing in his pad.)*

LYDIA. Read me *unas de tus* poems, Misha.

MISHA. Uh...sure.

LYDIA. Tonight.

*(She goes. **MISHA** exults.)*

CECI. Ghggng. Ghgng.

MISHA. You hear that, *carnala*? She wants my poems!

(He shuts off the TV and goes to her.)

CECI. Gh. Ghgngn.

(She points to the pen in his pocket.)

MISHA. Oh! You wanna poem. Okay. Ode to Ceci.

(He tries to write a poem in her palm, but he can't.)

Sorry, sis. All my poems come out for her. One for the way she laughs. One for the way she irons my pants. *Ayy.* Ten for the hurt that presses on me when she's near.

CECI. Where does it hurt?

MISHA. Mainly here. Pumping through my veins one single word. Lydia.... Lydia...Lydia....I can't think, I can't sleep. I curl up in bed and cry.

CECI. I hear you.

MISHA. Sis, have you ever felt this? I don't mean puppy crushes or shit like that. I mean, blind dumb love.

CECI. Blinder, dumber.

MISHA. Is it legal to want her this much? 'cause I want her.

CECI. Worker ant, don't do it.

MISHA. What if she doesn't like me? What if she just doesn't feel the same way I do?

CECI. Then hope to God she tells you, Meesh.

MISHA. Shit. You're lucky you don't have to deal with this anymore. Way too much hurt for the risk.

CECI. Lucky? I'm the opposite of lucky. If wanting to love and be loved back is lucky. I'm the opposite of luck, the opposite of possibility and love and Cecilia Rosario Florhhhggghn.

MISHA. I take it by your look you're saying I should go for it.

CECI. Ggggnh.

*(**CLAUDIO** enters again from his bedroom, a troubled look on his face. **MISHA** leaps up to take **CECI** off his La-Z-Boy and back to her mattress.)*

CLAUDIO. *¿Donde está Lydia?*

MISHA. Out with Mom.

CLAUDIO. *¿Cuando regresan?*

MISHA. No idea.

(He reaches into the cushions of his chair for his bottle. He takes a swig. He spits it out.)

CLAUDIO. *¡Que la Chingada Madre! ¡Cabrones!*

MISHA. *¿Que onda, Dad?* What's wrong?

CLAUDIO. *¿Quien puso* Wesson *en mi botella?*

MISHA. What?

CLAUDIO. Who put cooking oil *en mi botella*

MISHA. It wasn't me! I swear!

CLAUDIO. *Hijo de la chingada – !*

MISHA. I swear! I had nothing to do with that, Dad!

*(**CLAUDIO** raises his fist to strike him and **MISHA** cowers. He sees his son's terror. **MISHA** looks up at him and sees the same fear in his father's eyes. **CLAUDIO** turns away.)*

CLAUDIO. Get up. I know who did this.

MISHA. Who.

CLAUDIO. *¿Quien mas?* Rene. I don't lay my hand on him not since before *mija*, and see how he hates me.

*(**MISHA** disappears into the kitchen.)*

Nadie me escucha. Nobody listen to me. I'm nothing *en esta casa.* I work like a *negro* and still I nothing.

*(**MISHA** returns with a beer and offers it to **CLAUDIO**.)*

MISHA. It'll wash that greasy taste down.

*(**CLAUDIO** takes it and sips.)*

Is there anything else I can do?

CLAUDIO. No.

MISHA. Want me to take that for you?

*(**CLAUDIO** gives him the liquor bottle. Notices the pen in his breast pocket.)*

CLAUDIO. *¿Y eso, de donde chingaos viene?*

MISHA. Mom bought it. Half-price.

*(**CLAUDIO** nods. He sits in his chair. **MISHA** clicks on the TV and brings him his headphones.)*

CLAUDIO. *Eres un buen muchacho.* You are a decent boy. *Tu mama,* she raise you well.

*(***CLAUDIO** *puts on the headphones and stares at the TV.* **MISHA** *takes the bottle and starts to go back to his room. He stops.)*

MISHA. Dad?...*Jefe?*

(No response.)

For what it's worth, it wasn't just Mom who raised me. It was you, too, asshole. You're half to blame. You're the idiot who knocked her up, right? Your last name is mine, too, right? Everything about me you resent is half of you too, motherfucker. So take some credit, Dad. I'm your son. I'm your decent well-raised second son. You bred me with fists and belts and shoes and whatever else you could throw at me. You raised me to jump at the sound of your voice and the stamp of your foot. You taught me to cower and shake and cover my ears in bed at night so I wouldn't hear Mom screaming while you slapped her. You taught me shame. I should grow up to be a spiteful little fucker just like you, hating the world for the crap I bring on myself, piling some real hurt on the people who care for me most. Except you know what, I won't. No sir, I won't be you. I don't know what the hell I'm gonna be and god knows I may turn out worse than I think, but I won't be you. Some day, not today, against my better sense, I'm gonna forgive you. You'll see.

(He turns and goes. A pause. **CLAUDIO** *stands and goes to his stereo.)*

CLAUDIO. Next time put the needle on the record.

(He sits and watches TV. The glow from the TV intensifies, casting long shadows across the room. Then the lights brighten over **CECI**.*)*

CECI. How come, Daddy? How come you don't unload on him now? Is it 'cause he's right? Is it 'cause like Rene you crave to be punished? Or is it 'cause of Lydia?

Does it take a stranger to make you quit your *pendejadas*? I see you, the man inside the man who coulda been. All afternoon still as a lawn Mexican, you wait for the changes inside. You fall into a sleep that permits no dreaming, no dreaming on this side for you Apa….

*(**CLAUDIO** sleeps. A knock. **ALVARO** in his street clothes steps in. A bag draped over his arm.)*

ALVARO. *Tio? Tio* Claudio? Hello?

Hey Ceci. Your dad hibernates like a bear.

Oye. About last week. I haven't been the same since… well, since.

(He comes toward her. Touches her dress.)

That day I came over. You were wearing this.

CECI. I wanted to see what fifteen looked like.

ALVARO. But it wasn't finished yet. None of us were.

*(Some scratchy AM radio tune plays from somewhere down the hall. **ALVARO** hears it and then starts in its direction. Lights change. **CECI** stirs and calls.)*

CECI. VARO!

ALVARO. Hey Ceci! I heard the radio and – whoa! Lookit you!

CECI. What do you think? You like it?

ALVARO. Turn around. *Prima,* you look *fine*! Is it finished?

CECI. Almost. Just some hemming to do. Why are you looking at me like that?

ALVARO. I had no idea my cuz was such a fox. You're turning into a real beauty.

CECI. Hey, you better come to my *quinceañera.*

ALVARO. I'm there. I just can't get too messed up 'cause you know I'm shipping out the next morning.

CECI. I wish you didn't have go. Can't you get some exemption or something?

ALVARO. Actually, Ceci, I wanna go.

CECI. But why? Don't you watch the body counts on the news?

ALVARO. Sure I do. That's why I need to be there. My mom and dad, when they came over, they had nothing. Being American means a lot to them. C'mon, you know this. We got a flag on our porch.

CECI. But you're the brain of the family! You should be in college!

ALVARO. *Mira,* Ceci, the truth is, since graduation, I've felt like some discipline's gone AWOL in my life, and what better way to get it back than to do my duty *por Tío Sam?*

CECI. God, you are something. Varo, will you, like, be my first dance? At my *quinceañera?*

ALVARO. That's reserved for your father.

CECI. But after him, the next dance. Will you ask me, I mean, never mind, what am I thinking, huh?

ALVARO. Cecilia Rosario, may I have the honor of throwing some *chancla* with you?

(She smiles and offers her hand. They dance to some Temptations song on the radio.)*

CECI. I hope they play this song.

ALVARO. I'll see that they do. Anyways, is Rene home?

CECI. No, he's running some errands for Mom. What's up?

ALVARO. I gotta talk to that dude. There's something I gotta tell him.

CECI. Tell me. I'll tell him.

ALVARO. No, this is personal guy stuff, Ceci – .

CECI. Is it drugs?

ALVARO. What? No!

CECI. Are you guys toking up or something?

ALVARO. God, you been watching too much Mod Squad, *esa.* Just tell him I came by. Tell him I had to put my car in the shop.

CECI. Your car?

ALVARO. Tell him tonight's my only night. That's all. I gotta split. You're gonna kill 'em in this.

*See Music Use Note, Page 3.

(He turns to leave.)

CECI. Alvaro. Wait.

(She kisses him hard on the mouth. He is startled.)

ALVARO. Oh my god, Ceci –

(He kisses her back.)

CECI. I knew it. I knew you liked me. The first time at the Bronco Drive-in with you in the backseat with my brothers. I let my hand slip into yours under the blanket and you held it tight on your lap which was so warm. That's when I knew! *Te quiero, Alvaro. Te quiero mucho.* Oh my god, I can't believe what I'm saying!

ALVARO. Me neither –

CECI. I've come of age. I don't need no party to prove it. I know what I feel.

ALVARO. Ceci. You're my cousin.

CECI. Do you want me? That's all you have to say. Do you?

ALVARO. Tee-tee-tee. In ant language, that means you're the queen.

CECI. *(leaping into his arms)* I knew it! I knew it! Take me with you.

ALVARO. Take you…?

CECI. You and Rene taking dad's car and partying tonight, aren't you?

ALVARO. Oh shit. Rene.

CECI. Can I come? I won't be any trouble. It'll be fun, like the three of us at the drive-in.

ALVARO. No, Ceci, and you can't tell anybody this. It's guy's night out, that's all.

CECI. Please let me come. If you want me, you'll let me come.

(He kisses her long and deep. The lights change back. The radio fades. When **ALVARO** *pulls away,* **CECI** *is restored to her brain-damaged state.)*

Uhhhh uuh.

ALVARO. You shouldn't've come. You should've stayed home. It wasn't you. It was never you.

CLAUDIO. *Sobrino.*

(**CLAUDIO**, *awake for some time, takes off his headphones.)*

ALVARO. *Buenas noches. Disculpe sí lo desperté, tio.*

CLAUDIO. *¿Como se te parece? ¿Todavía bonita, que no?*

ALVARO. *Si, señor.* Still very pretty.

CLAUDIO. She is our penance. How we repay our *pecados.*

ALVARO. *Nos perdona Dios los pecados.*

CLAUDIO. In English, please. I learn.

ALVARO. God forgives our sins, Don Claudio. He doesn't take them out on others.

CLAUDIO. Mine, He does. What happen that night?

ALVARO. Sir? I don't understand...

CLAUDIO. All this time, I wonder where they go. To see you, *que no?*

ALVARO. *No señor.*

CLAUDIO. They come to your house, *verdad? Rene y Cecilia. Y tu.*

ALVARO. You know what happened, *Tío.*

CLAUDIO. I know what happen to *mija.* What happen to you? Why you no come see her the next day? They are going to see you, no? You are there *tambien, verdad?* What do you know about this accident? You can tell me, Varo. I won't hate you. I just want to know. *¡Contestame!*

ALVARO. What does it matter now? How's it going to change anything? She's not going to get better.

CECI. Oh no oh no. All my love wasted, all my wishing ruined, no chance of that cherry going boom.

ALVARO. You and me, *Tío, somos iguales.* Blaming ourselves for nothin'.

(**ROSA, LYDIA,** *and* **RENE** *burst through the front door with shopping bags.)*

ROSA. Alvaro! Praise the lord! What a surprise! *¡Mira, Rene, tu primo!*

RENE. Hey.

ALVARO. I just came over, you know....

*(***MISHA** *enters as* **LYDIA** *rushes to* **CECI** *with her shopping bags.)*

ROSA. We were shopping all day, sorry, *Viejo,* Lydia had never seen the mall, you know the new mall they put by the freeway! So I took her and you should have seen the look on her face!

LYDIA. It's the most beautiful place I have ever seen!

ROSA. We bought some things, *Viejo.*

LYDIA. I got some make-up and some perfume, see? And then I got some high-tone shampoo for my hair and conditioner, and some soap so I smell like Ali McGraw. And then at the Popular, I got these new shoes. See? *¿Les gustan mis zapatos?*

CLAUDIO. How did you pay for this?

ROSA. I advanced her for the month.

CLAUDIO. A month's pay to smell like a *gringa.*

LYDIA. Like a rich *gringa.*

ROSA. On the way home, we saw Rene walking on the street. So we picked him up, praise Jesus.

RENE. I wanted to walk.

ROSA. But look who you would miss if you did!

*(***LYDIA** *goes to* **CECI** *and puts some perfume on her wrist.)*

ALVARO. For you, cuz.

(He unzips the bag. A souvenir jacket with colored embroidery.)

ROSA. Oh! *¡Que bonito!* Goodness, look at the back! Ay, Rene...

(Sewn in gold lettering over an embroidered map of Indochina is written: "When I die, I am going to Heaven, because I've already done my time in Hell." **RENE** *puts it on.)*

ALVARO. Straight outa Vietnam, *ese.* I meant to bring it last time but I was having your name sewn on the inside seam.

RENE. What can I say? It's great.

ALVARO. Over there, Rene, family is everything. That's all that kept me going. I went over there for you, man. I know I made some choices in my job that don't sit well in this house, and I'm sorry. But we can't let that burn up the good times we had. I need you to accept what I am, 'cause you're my cousin and I love you.

RENE. What did you say?

ALVARO. You're my cousin.

RENE. No, you said something else. What did you say? Say it. Say it.

ALVARO. Rene, I'm doing the best I can –

RENE. SAY IT! You fucking hypocrite!

ROSA. RENE!

*(**RENE** scrambles for the door. **CLAUDIO** grabs his arm and he stops. They look at each other for the first time. **RENE** jerks his arm away and runs out.)*

CECI. Gggngng.

ROSA. *Lo siento.* Rene just can't get used to this INS business.

ALVARO. I understand, *Tia Rosa.* He'll come around.

LYDIA. Ceci says it is best that you go.

ALVARO. Your *criada* has a wild imagination, *Tia.* Ceci.

*(**ALVARO** goes.)*

ROSA. Did you see that, *Viejo*? Did you see how Rene was?

CLAUDIO. I saw.

ROSA. And you're not even going to ask him why?

CLAUDIO. Already a million times I ask him!

ROSA. *¡Por Dios santo!* Nobody make sense here! Rene! Rene!

*(She goes out after **RENE**. **MISHA** goes to his room. **LYDIA** and **CLAUDIO** regard each other in silence.)*

LYDIA. Are you going to stand there? He's your son, *viejo.*

CLAUDIO. Don't call me that. Only *Rosa* calls me that.

(**CLAUDIO** *stalks to the stereo and get his headphones.)*

LYDIA. He needs you.

CLAUDIO. *(putting them on and sitting in front of the TV)* Leave me alone.

LYDIA. Look at you. Locked inside your pride, while your family suffers.

(She rips the cord out of the stereo.)

Talk to him, Claudio!

CLAUDIO. How! How to take back all that time of not talking to him?

LYDIA. By talking to him. You men are so stubborn!

CLAUDIO. He look at me like I am a stranger.

LYDIA. You're his father.

CLAUDIO. All week, *sofocando.* I can't breathe. I'm dying.

LYDIA. You're not dying. The opposite.

CLAUDIO. You call this living?

LYDIA. She does. Your life is here, *hombre.*

(**CLAUDIO** *grabs his coat in agitation and starts out.)*

Are you going for Rene?

CLAUDIO. I'm going to work.

(He goes. She starts picking up the shopping bags.)

CECI. Gggggg.

LYDIA. *¿Ves, chica? Tanto desmadre aqui. Oye,* you know why we were out so late? Your *mami* couldn't say it in front of your cousin. We went to see someone in her building who is going to get me papers. She wants me to be legal.

CECI. *Ghhyyn?*

LYDIA. She wants my name in the passport to be Flores.

(She smiles and then goes. The lights change, brightening over **CECI.***)*

CECI. Flores is a name that goes all the way back to Spain, all the way back to the origin of flowers, which is what the name means. And the Flores that live in this town, all of them come from the first Flores that ever made love to an *India.* He gave her flowers for a name and she wore them for the next one and the next one wore them for the next one after that. All the way down to me. The pink icing on my cake said Flores. My wrist band said Flores. The red and white blooms in my head are Flores.

(The lights are out in the living room where **CECI** *lies.* **MISHA** *enters sheepishly.)*

MISHA. Ceci?

CECI. Gggnh, ggnh.

MISHA. I went in your room. It's all different now. She took your Bobby Sherman poster down. And all those Barbies you used to have. They're gone.

CECI. Ggnhh.

(He sits by her.)

MISHA. Sis, remember those summers when we were little and Dad used to take us to the community pool on his days off?

*(***LYDIA*** appears, in her bathrobe with a towel on her head, holding a manuscript.)*

MISHA. There was this one afternoon, when Rene was going up on the diving board and taking these big dives, and even at twelve, he was so graceful. And Dad's just standing in the water watching him like he's this god, and he says to me: I swam the Rio for this boy, I swam and ran straight to the hospital where your mother was giving birth and made sure his name was Claudio Rene Flores. I go, you can't swim, Dad. And he just goes, I know.

LYDIA. The shower is free if you need.

MISHA. I know. I heard Ceci and…I should let you get dressed.

LYDIA. Did *Señora* find your brother?

MISHA. Not yet.

LYDIA. You left this on my bed.

MISHA. You asked for my poems.

LYDIA. *(looking over them) Gracias.* Your sister and you, very close, no? You tell each other secrets.

MISHA. I do, anyway.

LYDIA. I bet she has some of her own. I like this one. *Sombra de Lydia.* Are you in love, young boy?

MISHA. I don't know what to do with girls. I never have.

LYDIA. You'll learn.

MISHA. Lydia, who are you? Why did you come here?

LYDIA. 'Cause I need work.

MISHA. But you're here for something else. I know.

LYDIA. You want my secrets now?

MISHA. I want to know everything about you. You're so far from your home and –

LYDIA. My home, Misha, *sinceramente,* is nowhere. What I had back in Mexico. It's all gone. I am hardly even here.

MISHA. What do you mean?

(She shows him a small mark on her chest.)

LYDIA. I died, Misha. Like Ceci, I died but I came back.

MISHA. Jesus. What is that?

LYDIA. My eyes were closed for a long time. When I opened them, I was an orphan.

MISHA. What happened?

LYDIA. It doesn't matter. This says I'm here now. This says I can't never go back.

MISHA. Are you a *mojada*? A wetback?

LYDIA. Uh-huh, but that's 'cause I just took a shower.

MISHA. Your English is getting better all the time.

LYDIA. *Gracias, guapo.* I practice with your sister all day.

MISHA. You're good with her. She needs you.

LYDIA. It's you she needs. *En serio.* She counts on your poetry. *Un dia,* when you are alone, look into her *ojitos* and hold her hand tight, don't let go, no matter what.

MISHA. I don't understand.

LYDIA. I'm saying give her love and she will give you all the *poemas* of her life. *Para siempre.* Can I keep?

MISHA. They're all for you.

(He slowly moves in to kiss her. She lets him.)

LYDIA. Misha…

(He kisses her again. His hand slides into her bathrobe. She likes it, but has to resist it.)

See how quickly you learn.

MISHA. I'm just down the hall.

LYDIA. That's how it has to stay, sweet boy.

(She kisses his cheek, then he goes. **LYDIA** *reads his poems, tears welling in her eyes.)*

CECI. *Ay Lydia.* All the want of before, dilating my *corazón,* it's dilating yours. You speak the *idioma* of ants and miscarried love. The cards of *La Vida Cecilia* falling into place. Some *desmadre* is coming into view and I'm gonna need you, *loca.* I'll need you when I fall.

LYDIA. *¿Que ves, pajarita?*

CECI. A new card. *Las Gemelas.* The twins.

*(***LYDIA** *goes. Darkness descends on the living room.* **ROSA** *sits on the sofa in her nightgown.)*

ROSA. Dear Jesus. I know Rene won't amount to much, that's what I believe, that's my sin, to dismiss my oldest so easily. He'll be a loyal son if he lives to be twenty. But he won't make a difference in the world. I know it, he knows it and You know it too. But that don't mean I don't love him. Bring him home tonight dear Father –

*(***RENE** *can be heard roaring outside, crashing against garbage cans.)*

RENE. *(off) ¡Chinga la verga! ¡Pinchi puto cabron!* Who do you think you are! I got every right to be here!

*(***ALVARO** *enters pushing* **RENE** *inside. He drunkenly staggers in, his hands cuffed behind him.)*

Let go of me! I said, LET ME GO!

ALVARO. Shut up, Rene! You're gonna wake the whole block!

RENE. You can't treat me like this! I ain't your wetback! You don't get rid of me that easy, you shit!

ALVARO. I know what you're trying to do. It's not gonna work.

RENE. You don't get it, do you! You drivin' to the levee, right by the same fuckin' pole! That's why you joined *la Migra*!

ALVARO. What do you want from me!

RENE. I want you to talk to me! Jesus Christ, just talk to me!

ALVARO. There's nothin' to talk about! I'm through, that's all!

RENE. Then why did you give me your jacket? If you hate my guts so much, why!

ALVARO. Listen up, you fuck! You were part of my war! The whole time I was there, so were you! What we had, *ese*, nobody's ever gonna touch that, nobody's ever gonna come that close! That was it, *ese*. That was my shot.

RENE. Then why won't you see me, goddammit!

ALVARO. 'Cause when I think of us, I see her! I hear those words!

RENE. What are you sayin', asshole? I live with her! I hear them every day!

ROSA. Rene. *¿Que es esta locura?*

ALVARO. He was up on the levee, *Tia*. He's drunk. He taunted us while we were doing our job.

RENE. Oh my god! You were buying me off! This jacket's to buy me off!

ALVARO. He's talking like a crazy man.

ROSA. *Mijo,* please don't be like this….

RENE. Get the fuck away! I'm done with you.

(**MISHA** *enters in his tee-shirt and shorts.)*

MISHA. Mom, back away.

ROSA. *¡Pero, mijo, mira que locura!*

RENE. *¡Carnalito!*

MISHA. Do as I say. Back away.

(**ROSA** *retreats in sobs as* **RENE** *grows more glowering and furious.* **CECI** *becomes agitated.)*

RENE. That's right! Back away from the Fag Basher!

MISHA. What the hell are you doing, man?

RENE. Don't look at me like that, Meesh! I'll fuckin' bust your head open! Like I busted Ceci!

MISHA. What can I do, Rene? *Te quiero ayudar.* Tell me what to do.

CECI. GGNNGAYAAYYY!!

RENE. Hypocrites and liars! I fuckin' hate you all!

ALVARO. Misha, he just needs to sleep it off. *(to* **RENE***)* You gotta get a grip.

RENE. FUCK YOU! TAKE THESE OFF AN' LEMME KICK YOUR ASS, YOU FUCKING COWARD!

(**LYDIA** *appears.)*

LYDIA. *¿Que pasa aqui?*

RENE. *Orale.* You want an illegal? You wanna do your fuckin'job, *migra?*

MISHA. Go back to your room.

LYDIA. Let me take Ceci out.

ROSA. Take her to your room. *Andale.*

RENE. Don't put your dirty hands on her. *Mojada.*

MISHA. Rene…

RENE. I'm telling you, cuz, this one's trouble. This one thinks she knows our shit. She's gone real deep with us, *verdad, criada?*

MISHA. Back away from her. I mean it.

RENE. It's sad, *ese.* You giving your heart to a wetback. She's using you!

MISHA. I don't care. I'm not letting you say whatever you want about her.

ROSA. *¡Misha, cuidado, mijo!*

RENE. You think she's *toda India Mexicana.* But I've seen Dad banging this whore!

ROSA. Lydia…

(**MISHA** *pounds him in the gut and he falls.)*

Misha!

MISHA. I TOLD YOU TO WATCH YOUR MOUTH!

RENE. I saw them!

MISHA. Liar!

(He grabs **RENE** *by the collar and threatens to hit him.)*

ALVARO. STOP IT!

RENE. C'mon, bro. C'mon. Just lemme have it. Just pound on me, man.

(**MISHA** *lets him go.)*

¡Andale, Miguel! ¡Dale gas! Hit me, motherfucker! I want you to hit me!

MISHA. No way….

RENE. *(collapsing in tears.)* ALVARO! ANY A YOU! I'M BEGGIN' YOU! JESUS, SOMEBODY FUCKIN HIT ME!

ALVARO. Jesus, Rene, quit this now please….

(**CECI** *convulses in terror and* **LYDIA** *runs to holds her tightly.* **MISHA** *looks at* **ALVARO**.*)*

MISHA. Are you going to tell us what is going on here? Will somebody tell us?

CECI. Ghhhn.

LYDIA. She will.

ALVARO. What?

MISHA. What are you talking about?

CECI. Ghghggn.

LYDIA. She knows. She was there.

CECI. Ghgn.

LYDIA. She is there now.

ROSA. She is?

CECI. Gghfnhsss

LYDIA. She says Rene and me

CECI. Ggffeggh-ghfhn

LYDIA. Driving in the middle of the night

CECI. Gghaagg

LYDIA. To Alvaro's house

CECI. Ttte-tttteee

LYDIA. Delirious as ants

CECI. Ghhhngnn

LYDIA. Rene is driving

CECI. Hhghhhh.

LYDIA. But I'm hiding in the backseat. Crouched in the floor of the backseat.

CECI. 'Cause I wanna surprise them! I wanna see the look on Alvaro's face when he sees me again! Party!

LYDIA. She says

CECI. I hear the radio playing and I feel the wind rushing in through his open window and I'm tingling with excitement! I'm gonna trip 'em out!

LYDIA. She says

CECI. I hear the car stop and Alvaro getting in and I'm about to jump out, but he's like on Rene, kissing him, and my heart stops and

LYDIA. She says

CECI. I can't think I can't move but the car does. It rolls along at Roadrunner speed to nowhere and I can hear them talking Rene's like where you wanna go and Alvaro's like where we always go, cuz, the border

LYDIA. She says

CECI. I'm *toda* dizzy. But soon, I feel the car stopping. The engine stops and it's quiet as death

LYDIA. *Quiet as death*

CECI. I feel the beautiful dream of Varo and me slipping away as I hear this moaning and kissing and crying

LYDIA. She says

CECI. This moaning and kissing and crying

LYDIA. She says

CECI. And then I see Alvaro throw his head back and cry out

LYDIA. *¡Ay Rene!*

CECI. I see *carnal* rise up and kiss him and I can't believe it

LYDIA. She says

CECI. Alvaro was mine all these years I dreamed of kissing him like that and now

LYDIA. She says

CECI. Right there, right there, this ugliness inside takes over: YOU FAGS. YOU HOMOS. YOU DIRTY FILTHY HOMOS

LYDIA. She says

CECI. They scream, they're so shocked but the ugly keeps yelling You *Jotos,* Damn *Maricones.* Rene starts the car and says over and over

RENE. Don't tell Dad, Ceci, please don't tell Dad

CECI. And Varo's face turned away saying

ALVARO. We weren't doing nothing, I swear

CECI. And the car is racing and I'm screaming in the backseat YOU DISGUST ME YOU MAKE ME SICK YOU LYING SHITS

LYDIA. She says

CECI. I'm beating on Rene, I am so mad at Rene. And he's yelling No and Alvaro is yelling Stop, Ceci! But my fists keep hitting his head and the car is swerving like crazy, and Rene reaches back and tells me right to my face

LYDIA. I'm sorry!

CECI. But he's not looking and the curve is right there and the pole wants the Pontiac. And there in the rear-view mirror I see you, so pale and sad, the face of death willing the car into the pole

LYDIA. Just as I see yours in my mirror

CECI. And I am pure bird soaring with the moon stretching out like *chicle* toward the red card with the inscription: Now Look What You Done, Stupid

LYDIA. She says

CECI. It was me! ME! This *mierda* was me! You didn't do nothing wrong! It was all my shit my fucking shit making it wrong. The words in my heart fall out the crack in my head. The words I never meant this. Not in a million. I love you Rene. I love you both. I'm ssgh-ggngn..ggngn.

LYDIA. *Eso es lo que dice.*

(Silence. **ALVARO** *takes the cuffs off* **RENE.***)*

ROSA. Is it true? Alvaro.

ALVARO. No, *Tia.*

ROSA. Rene? Is it true, Rene?

RENE. Yeah. All true.

ROSA. Get out. Get out of this house.

MISHA. Mom, you can't just –

RENE. *Aliviánate, carnal.* I'm done here.

(He takes off the jacket and throws it at **ALVARO***'s feet. Then he goes to* **CECI** *to make his goodbye. Intimate and silent. Then he gets up and walks out of the house forever.)*

LYDIA. *(as she gets up and starts to her room)* She wants to rest now. I'm tired too.

MISHA. Were you…did you and my dad…?

LYDIA. What importance is that now, Misha?

(She goes. **MISHA** *looks at* **ROSA.***)*

ROSA. I always say nothing happens in this house without me knowing. But really, all I knew was nothing.

MISHA. Mom, you can't let him go like that.

ROSA. Go to bed, *mijo.*

(**MISHA** *goes.* **ALVARO** *makes to go but* **ROSA** *stops him.)*

Sobrino.

(**ROSA** *goes to him and whispers something to him as* **CECI** *cowers on her mattress.)*

CECI. This *noche* nobody sleeps. This *noche* the words slam against the walls like angry little birds again and again. Faggot. Whore. *Mojado. Migra. Mijo.* Love. All these words on razor wings looking for something to cut. Slashing at the walls of what we used to call family.

(**ALVARO** *nods gravely to* **ROSA**. *He goes down the hall.* **ROSA** *sits with* **CECI**.*)*

ROSA. What does the word *madre* mean in this country? Does it mean idiot? Does it mean pretending? Does it mean living like nothing's changed? Everything's changed. I'm old. I'm a stranger to my own children. My husband won't touch me. You were going to be my partner, but look at you.

CECI. Gnnghg.

(There is an awful lull, then screaming and yelling off.)

LYDIA. *(off)* AAAYYY! AAAAAYYYY!

(**ALVARO** *enters dragging* **LYDIA** *out behind him.)*

ALVARO. That's the way it is. Now come on!

LYDIA. *AYYY! AYY! Help me!*

(**MISHA** *comes out.)*

MISHA. Whoa! What the fuck are you doing?

LYDIA. *Misha!* He's taking me away!

ALVARO. She's got no proof of residence, cuz.

MISHA. What! Where are you taking her?

ALVARO. Where do you think? *El Corralón.*

LYDIA. *Señora*! Tell him I'm American! He won't listen to me! I'm American!

ROSA. *Es una mojada.* I don't hire *mojadas.*

ALVARO. *Vamonos.*

MISHA. Mom, you can't do this. I won't let you.

ROSA. You dare defend her in my presence? *Esta degraciada se abusó de mi marido,* my husband!

LYDIA. *Señora,* please, don't be this way! I love this family! Misha!

MISHA. Let her go, Varo. C'mon, for family, cuz.

ALVARO. *Misha, con esto, familia no vale madre.*

LYDIA. *¡Misha, por favor!* I don't want to go back! If I go back, I'll die! I know I will. I'll die!

ROSA. Alvaro Fernandez. TAKE THIS *PUTA* OUT OF MY HOUSE NOW!

ALVARO. C'mon.

LYDIA. Wait! My poems! Let me get my poems! Misha!

ROSA. *Espera.*

*(**ROSA** violently strips off **LYDIA**'s top.)*

LYDIA. NOO!

ROSA. This is *Mija's blusa.*

LYDIA. CECI! CECI!

*(**ALVARO** pushes **LYDIA**, ravaged and half-naked, out the door.)*

MISHA. I love her.

ROSA. *Mira nomas.* Her little *pendejito.* Writing *mierda* to her with my pen.

*(**MISHA** runs out after **LYDIA**. **ROSA** sits in exhaustion. The lights collapse in around **CECI**.)*

CECI. I flew that night to a village in Jalisco; through a window, this girl sitting at a dresser brushing her hair. She looks in the mirror, sees me and smiles like she's always known me, this tragic girl brushing her hair at the break of day.

*(Later in the morning. **CLAUDIO** enters carrying a paper bag filled with take-out. He finds **CECI** and **ROSA** sleeping together on the mattress.)*

CLAUDIO. *Vieja.* Rosa.

ROSA. Hmm?

*(***ROSA** *wakes.)*

CLAUDIO. *¿Que haces? ¿Porque duermes aqui?*

ROSA. I got lonely.

CLAUDIO. I brought you some *menudo.*

ROSA. *Gracias.*

CLAUDIO. *¿Esta todo bien? (She nods.) ¿Y Rene?* Did *mijo* come back home?

ROSA. He's still out.

CLAUDIO. I will talk to him. *Pos,* you better have some before it gets cold.

(She opens the container of menudo. **CLAUDIO** *takes a beer from his bag and pops off the pull-tab.)*

CECI. Gghnf.

CLAUDIO. *Qiubolé, mija.* Are you ever going to change out of that thing? Uh?

CECI. Da..hh…da..ghgntttee.

CLAUDIO. *Querida.* The only English I want to know is yours.

(He kisses her forehead, but forgets the pull-tab on her blanket.)

ROSA. I love when they put extra *tripas.* Menudo is always good for the morning-after.

CLAUDIO. Are you hung-over?

ROSA. *Hombre,* this headache like a devil with a claw hammer. I think I'm staying in today.

CLAUDIO. Then lie down for a while. *¿Y Lydia?*

ROSA. *Se fue.*

CLAUDIO. *¿Como que se fue?* Where is she?

ROSA. *Con la Migra.*

CLAUDIO. *¿Que chingados dices, mujer?* You turn her over to *La Migra?*

ROSA. If you want her, *vete.* If you miss that fucking country so much, go. Let me remind you who also needs papers.

(They glare at each other. Then **CLAUDIO** *retreats to his bedroom. He stops at the threshold.)*

CLAUDIO. Rene and Cecilia…*y* Alvaro. Why?

ROSA. There is no why. There is never any why.

*(***MISHA** *enters dressed. He goes straight to* **CECI** *and begins her physical therapy.)*

CLAUDIO. Miguel….Miguel…

(No response. He turns to **ROSA.***)*

Come to bed. Bring the menudo with you.

*(***CLAUDIO** *goes.* **ROSA** *can stomach no more soup. She goes to Miguel. She looks at* **CECI.***)*

ROSA. *¿Y tu que ves?* What other *cochinadas* are locked in those pretty eyes of yours?

(She walks solemnly down the hall.)

CECI. Gggighg.

MISHA. It's okay, sis. I know you didn't mean it.

CECI. Mmmm…. Meeesh shhhhhah!

MISHA. Sis, did you just – ?

CECI. Mmmeeshishhhh. Aaah.

(He goes to her and she kisses his hand.)

MISHA. Oh my god. Ceci. You're talking.

(She guides his hand under her dress.)

Wait…what are you…no…. let go. Please, Ceci. Let go! I'm sorry. No.

(He breaks away. She curls up and cries softly. He tries to leave but stops at the threshold of the room. He turns and crawls along invisible trails toward his sister.)

In ant-language, teetee means sister. In ant, teeteetee means touch. I wish I knew the word for Ceci.

CECI. Tee- teeeh.

MISHA. I hear you.

(He crawls to her.)

In my dream, you had a key in your mouth.

*(**CECI** finds the pull-tab and shows it to him.)*

CECI. My magic key out of ant-prison, forged from Daddy's pull-tab.

MISHA. I love you, Ceci.

CECI. Aayyyhhh.

(He grits his teeth as she moves his hand into her. She begins to feel him as he cries.)

The last card. Inscribed, *Ay Te Watcho.* Which is God-speed in Chicano. So wave bye to me, little brother, and reach inside and spell the word love in a girl that's never felt it with your fingers push back the veil *ay, asi, carnal, asi,* find the poems in me 'cause I hid them all for you, *asi, asi,* poems of your hunger your shame your secret loves, *ay,* got them right here, Misha, your *versos –*

CECI/MISHA. – dancing in me, drowning in my blood –

MISHA. – reaching all the way up to your heart, I'll find the Ceci you'll never be, give you wings with my pen, make you fly, I'll be your poet forever, *con safo, retacho, asi asi Ceci dame la vida Cecilia asi*

CECI. *hhhhhhg.*

*(**MISHA** cries. **CECI**, in a spasm of ecstacy, sets the pull-tab gingerly on her tongue and swallows it. He watches her slowly slip away.)*

(lights fade)

End of Play

MUSIC AND THIRD PARTY MATERIALS USE NOTE

IMPORTANT BILLING AND CREDIT REQUIREMENTS

CPSIA information can be obtained
at www.ICGtesting.com
Printed in the USA
LVHW080336010922
727354LV00014B/1007

9 780573 698163